Hope for the Best

By:

Brooke St. James

No part of this book may be used or reproduced in any form or by any means without prior written permission of the author.

Other titles available from Brooke St. James:

Another Shot:
(A Modern-Day Ruth and Boaz Story)

When Lightning Strikes

Something of a Storm (All in Good Time #1)
Someone Someday (All in Good Time #2)

Finally My Forever (Meant for Me #1)
Finally My Heart's Desire (Meant for Me #2)
Finally My Happy Ending (Meant for Me #3)

Shot by Cupid's Arrow

Dreams of Us

Meet Me in Myrtle Beach (Hunt Family #1)
Kiss Me in Carolina (Hunt Family #2)
California's Calling (Hunt Family #3)
Back to the Beach (Hunt Family #4)
It's About Time (Hunt Family #5)

Loved Bayou (Martin Family #1)
Dear California (Martin Family #2)
My One Regret (Martin Family #3)
Broken and Beautiful (Martin Family #4)
Back to the Bayou (Martin Family #5)

Almost Christmas

JFK to Dublin (Shower & Shelter Artist Collective #1)
Not Your Average Joe (Shower & Shelter Artist Collective #2)
So Much for Boundaries (Shower & Shelter Artist Collective #3)
Suddenly Starstruck (Shower & Shelter Artist Collective #4)
Love Stung (Shower & Shelter Artist Collective #5)
My American Angel (Shower & Shelter Artist Collective #6)

Summer of '65 (Bishop Family #1)
Jesse's Girl (Bishop Family #2)
Maybe Memphis (Bishop Family #3)
So Happy Together (Bishop Family #4)
My Little Gypsy (Bishop Family #5)
Malibu by Moonlight (Bishop Family #6)
The Harder They Fall (Bishop Family #7)
Come Friday (Bishop Family #8)
Something Lovely (Bishop Family #9)

So This is Love (Miami Stories #1)
All In (Miami Stories #2)
Something Precious (Miami Stories #3)

The Suite Life (The Family Stone #1)
Feels Like Forever (The Family Stone #2)
Treat You Better (The Family Stone #3)
The Sweetheart of Summer Street (The Family Stone #4)
Out of Nowhere (The Family Stone #5)

Delicate Balance (Blair Brothers #1)
Cherished (Blair Brothers #2)
The Whole Story (Blair Brothers #3)
Dream Chaser (Blair Brothers #4)

Kiss & Tell (Novella) (Tanner Family #0)
Mischief & Mayhem (Tanner Family #1
Reckless & Wild (Tanner Family #2)
Heart & Soul (Tanner Family #3)
Me & Mister Everything (Tanner Family #4)
Through & Through (Tanner Family #5)
Lost & Found (Tanner Family #6)
Sparks & Embers (Tanner Family #7)
Young & Wild (Tanner Family #8)

Easy Does It (Bank Street Stories #1)
The Trouble with Crushes (Bank Street Stories #2)
A King for Christmas (Novella) (A Bank Street Christmas)
Diamonds Are Forever (Bank Street Stories #3)
Secret Rooms and Stolen Kisses (Bank Street Stories #4)
Feels Like Home (Bank Street Stories #5)
Just Like Romeo and Juliet (Bank Street Stories #6)
See You in Seattle (Bank Street Stories #7)
The Sweetest Thing (Bank Street Stories #8)
Back to Bank Street (Bank Street Stories #9)

Split Decision (How to Tame a Heartbreaker #1)
B-Side (How to Tame a Heartbreaker #2)

Cole for Christmas

Somewhere in Seattle (Alexander Family #1)
Wildest Dream (Alexander Family #2)
About to Fall (Alexander Family #3)

Hope for the Best (Morgan Family #1)

Chapter 1

Hope Jones
***
Graham Springs, Arkansas

"The Morgans are back in town," Stacy said.

For so many years, that was a normal thing for her to say, so I tuned her out. The Morgans used to come to Arkansas twice a year like clockwork. I would see them every summer and Christmas. The phrase was something I had heard Stacy say tons of times.

We grew up in a small lakeside town in the foothills of the Ozark mountains. Graham Springs was situated on the third largest lake in Arkansas—Lake Sutton. The lake was shaped a bit like the letter T that was kind of lying on its side. It was only sixty-five miles wide, but it was jagged and lopsided, and because of its odd shape, had almost four hundred miles of shoreline.

Graham Springs was among several tiny towns that bordered Lake Sutton. It was on the southeastern side of the lake, and it was the largest of all the lakeside towns, but it was still really small. We were home to seven thousand full-time residents and there were another two or three thousand around the lake who used our town seasonally during the summer. Graham Springs was far from a booming metropolis, but we had public schools, a department store, a few grocery stores, and a small hospital, which was more than any of our neighboring lakeside towns could say.

The main roadway looked like any other small town, but you could drive one minute toward the lake, and suddenly you were in the middle of pristine nature at its finest. Lake Sutton was God's country, with cliffs, trails, and waterfalls. There were picturesque views on every square mile of this lake.

I had been raised here, so I was used to the glory and splendor of it all, but I had also traveled to other states and cities, and I knew how rare and beautiful Lake Sutton was. During the peak traveling seasons, Lake Sutton was a vacation spot for rich people, so we had well-to-do seasonal guests during the holidays and summer.

That was how my mom met my dad. She grew up in Graham Springs, and my dad had come on vacation with a friend. He fell in love with my mother, and he wound up staying here that summer and never going back to Mississippi. They had me, and then my little brother came along a year later. My parents stayed together for a few years, but they weren't happy as a couple.

My dad stayed in the Lake Sutton area after they divorced, and my childhood was split going back and forth between the two of them. My little brother, Eric, came with me wherever I went, and I became a caretaker for him even though I was only a year older.

For ten years during our childhood, our dad lived in Broken Arrow and worked for the Morgan family.

Those were the best days.

The Morgan grandparents lived at the mansion full-time, and the children and grandchildren visited twice a year or more. Broken Arrow was further north and west in the upper portion of the letter T. It was around thirty miles from Graham Springs by car, or twenty by boat. I knew the two most direct routes like the back of my hand because I had traveled to the Morgans' lake house many times.

My father had worked for that family for ten years doing groundskeeping, yardwork, cleaning, painting, and other general maintenance. He wasn't the only person who worked for them, but he was the only one to live on the property full-time. During his time with the Morgan family, he lived in one of the three detached houses on the property—the one that was a little farther away from the others and was built specifically for the groundskeeper. I was with my dad about half of the time when he worked there. Legally, he only had custody of Eric and me two weekends out of the month, but we loved it at the Morgans' property, so we stayed with my dad as much as he would have us.

Those were the good old days. I lived in a tiny apartment with my mom in Graham Springs half the time and in Broken Arrow at a gorgeous mansion for the other half. Granted, Dad didn't live in the main house—but Eric and I got invited to go inside anytime the grandkids were visiting.

I had the sweetest, fondest memories of the Morgan family and their lake house. I was thrust into a moment of nostalgia when Stacy said their name, and it took a minute for her words to sink in.

"Wait, who's back?" I asked in a shocked tone since it had been years since I had heard their name.

"The Morgans," Stacy repeated, nodding. "They're back in town."

Several different thoughts and feelings hit me all at once, and Charlie Morgan was the first of them.

Maximus Charles Morgan Junior aka Charlie.

I thought of Charlie Morgan and pictured a sequence of nostalgic moments that I had shared with that boy. There were five or six guys in the Morgan-slash-Cameron clan, and they were all good-looking, but Charlie was the one I always had a crush on. I remembered curling up on the couch with him in the upstairs playroom when we were in middle school. We had watched The Goonies together fifty times, and I had amazing memories of lazy afternoons after hours of playing and swimming in the sun.

"Hope, are you even listening to me?"

"Yes, I am."

"I said the Morgans are here."

"The *Morgan*-Morgans?" I asked in disbelief. "I thought they… I thought that house was sold… abandoned."

Stacy shrugged as she wiped the tables next to me and adjusted the menus and napkins.

We were at her parents' restaurant. It was a small but longstanding pub in Graham Springs, a block away from the lake. It was everything all in one—a coffee shop, restaurant, and bar. The Black Skillet Inn. They served bar food like burgers, fries, sandwiches, and quesadillas—nothing fancy. But it was delicious, and there was not much else in town, so it was always busy. Stacy's parents had owned it since we were kids. She tried to escape the inevitability of working there, and she got a job at the bank when we graduated high school, but it didn't take. She was really good at working at the restaurant, and her parents loved having her around.

"I talked to them about it earlier," she said.

"Talked to who?" I asked, unable to process the fact that the Morgans were back in town.

"The Morgans," she said. "Mister Donnie and a few of the boys came in earlier. Beck and Casey were there, and Beau. I talked to them about the house."

"Casey was here? Is Charlie here?" I asked.

Charlie and Casey were brothers. They had a third brother named Caleb—the Florida boys, as we called them. "Charlie wasn't with them today, but I asked about him for you. They said he's here."

"He is? He's here? What's going on? Why are they back?"

I helped her by organizing the condiment and napkin holders on nearby tables. But I was curious about Charlie. My heart was racing, and he was nowhere in sight. I glanced around the dining room just to make sure.

Stacy continued with what she was saying. "I guess their grandpa died a few months ago, and that's what made them come back to the house. The lady, his wife, Miss Naomi had passed away eight years ago, remember? That's what made him move out of the house in the first place. He's been in Houston with Donnie and Sarah this whole time."

I knew Donnie and Sarah were Beck and Lila's parents. They were the Houston crew. The Houston crew had the last name Morgan and so did the Florida boys, but there was a Chicago bunch as well—the Camerons. Astrid Morgan had married film producer Danny Cameron and they had three kids, so three of the cousins were Camerons instead of Morgans. There were eight grandkids in total. I had spent many holidays with them, and I knew them well.

"I didn't know Mister Morgan had been living in Houston this whole time," I said distractedly as I thought of everything.

"That's what Donnie said," she answered. "They said he wouldn't sell the house, but that he wouldn't come up here either. He stopped using it, and it just stayed empty for the last eight years."

"Yeah, I remember hearing about Brandon Hall trying to use the swimming pool and getting caught," I said.

"That was a few years ago, I remember that," she said. "Josh told me they used the pool for months before they got caught. Brandon's dad had that pool company and they stole a bunch of his chemicals, remember?"

"I remember that," I said, nodding.

"They've had surveillance at the house since then, but none of the family visits. I don't think Mister Don wanted them to. Anyway, he passed away a few months ago, and they've had crews there renovating. They're all spending the summer here—meeting, working, deciding what to do with the property. Beck said it was thirty acres."

I nodded absentmindedly since I already knew how large it was. "Yeah. That's crazy. I can't believe they're all coming back. What do they look like?"

"Uh, gorgeous. A few of them have social media—Beck, AJ, and Rose. I don't think any of the Florida boys have it though. I looked them all up."

None of this was news to me. I had thought of them in recent years and searched for them. From the age of four through fourteen, the Morgans and Camerons were such a big part of my childhood memories that I couldn't help but be curious about how they all turned out.

"What does Casey look like?" I asked, wishing I had seen them today.

"Amazing," she said. "Like the guy who stars in that surfing movie. He looks just like he used to except grown up and hotter now."

I smiled and shook my head at her, and she laughed.

"He is. They all are. Beck's really good-looking too. And he's on social media. I easily found his stuff because he's famous. He's a painter. He's got like eighty thousand followers on Instagram."

"I know," I said.

"Rose Cameron has a bunch of pictures on her feed, too," Stacy added. "She has some with her brothers on there. AJ plays lacrosse. I think he and Beau both do, but Beau isn't on social media as far as I can tell."

"You sure do know a lot about the Morgans," I said.

Stacy shrugged. "I looked them all up after they came in here earlier."

"When was it?"

"A couple of hours ago," she said.

I glanced at the clock to find that it was a quarter after five. I worked the reception desk at a pediatrician's office, and I had just gotten off. I was hungry, and I had come straight to the restaurant to grab something for dinner. I stopped by here a few times a week because Stacy's family gave me food at cost and they kept a running tab which I paid once a month. Stan, Stacy's dad, was already working on my order in the kitchen.

"I didn't see Charlie earlier when the others came in, but I see him now."

Stacy continued cleaning and made the statement so casually that I looked at her with a confused expression. She smiled at me and pointed at the window like he was about to walk in.

"You're joking," I said staring at her and feeling like I might pass out.

"I'm not," she said, shaking her head at me with a wide-eyed expression. "He's about to—*Hey, welcome to The Black Skillet Inn*," Stacy said, calling toward the door.

"Thank you," a deep voice called back.

It took me a second, but I finally broke eye contact with Stacy and looked that way.

Chapter 2

Charlie.

The man version of Charlie Morgan stood in the doorway of Stacy's restaurant, and he was a sight to behold. He was too big for this establishment. Both of them were. Caleb came in first and—wait—there were three of them. Lila was standing behind Charlie, and I had been unable to see her because the boys were that big now. Caleb and Charlie were brothers and their cousin, Lila (from Houston), was with them.

I straightened my posture as I took in the threesome. It had been so long. They were dressed casually in jeans. They had been on a boat—I could tell by the things they were wearing and the general windblown look of their hair and clothes.

"It's been a while, Morgan family," Stacy said in her restaurant tone.

How was she able to act normal in front of them? She walked toward them while I peeled my eyes away from Charlie and finished adjusting the napkin holder.

"I saw your dad in here a little while ago," she continued, talking to Lila.

"That's why we came," Lila said. "Dad came home talking about how good this mushroom swiss burger still was, and we were like *where's ours*?"

"So, Lila took orders and now we need a catering van basically."

"It's not so bad," Lila said. "We need ten burgers."

"Oh, yeah, that's not so many," Stacy said. "Do you want me to go ahead and put in your order, or do you need a minute to look at a menu?"

"We'll come in and sit down," Caleb said.

"Yeah, I forgot how much I loved this place," Charlie added, looking around. "Hope, is that you?" He caught sight of me and figured out who I was after only a few seconds. I was so relieved that he remembered me.

"Yeah, I thought that was Hope," Lila said, coming toward me.

"I was thinking we knew her, too," Caleb added.

"Her dad used to work for Grandpa and Nonnie," Lila said. "Remember? She was at the house all the time."

"Oh, yeah," Caleb added, pointing and nodding at me.

It wasn't busy in the restaurant, and I walked toward them. Lila reached out like she was going to hug me, so I went to her. "Heyyy," she said. She looked me over. "Some things never change, huh? I never dreamed we'd come back here and find you in this same… are you a nurse?" she asked, pausing and looking at my scrubs.

"Oh, no, I'm a… I work at a pediatrician's office."

"Oh, that's cool," Lila said, being friendly.

I had stepped next to Charlie and he reached out to hug me. "What's up, Hope? How are you?"

"I'm good," I answered, stepping back. "Well," I added (since they always seemed so fancy and proper). "Doing well." I nodded and stepped back, trying to be casual. "How are you guys?"

They walked toward the counter, and Charlie looked at me like he expected me to follow them. "We're great," he said. "We just got here this morning. It's been a looong time."

"Eight years," Lila said. "We had a bunch of people over at the house working for the last month. Has your dad been helping with that?"

"Oh, no, he's working here, in Graham Springs at… the… hardware store… Ace." I regretted feeling the need to tell them exactly where he worked, but I was nervous.

"That's good, Ace is the place," Charlie said.

"Yeah, Charlie might know him if he worked at Ace Hardware in Miami."

"Do you work at Ace?" I asked.

I regretted asking it the instant he started shaking his head.

"He owns a construction company," Lila explained.

"Our dad helped me get that going," Charlie said. "And we mainly deal with a local place. But I shop at Ace all the time on weekends. If your dad worked at the one in Miami, I would probably see him all the time."

"He works at the one in Graham Springs," I said.

"That's cool," Charlie replied.

I followed them toward the counter. I hesitated to sit with them, so I hovered for a second. "I'm waiting on food from the kitchen," I explained.

"Oh, come sit with us," Charlie said.

Lila had darted ahead of everyone, and Charlie was the last in line, so we sat next to each other by default. I hated that I had my hair in a ponytail and had been at work all day.

"Weren't you named after a character on a daytime drama?" Lila asked, leaning behind the two guys to speak to me.

"Yes," I said, nodding.

"And your brother, too?" she asked.

I nodded. "Eric," I agreed. "Both of us are Days of our Lives characters."

"I knew it," she said. "Was it Hope and Eric Brady? I did research on that show."

"It is the Bradys," I said, smiling at her. "What kind of research?"

"I'm trying to get into acting, and my dad knows the producer of General Hospital. He's a patient at my dad's real hospital. My dad's helping me get my foot in the door with him."

"Oh, that one's been on a long time," I said. "My grandma used to watch it when I was a little girl. It's pretty good. You should try to get on there if your dad knows someone."

"Days is good, too. I've done some research on them lately and done a lot of watching. For like five hours a day, I just devour old episodes."

"That's cool. Just to practice?"

"Yeah, and to see what I like and I don't like about different actors. I'm sure I won't get a big role at first, but I'll try anything."

"You definitely should try for that," I said. "You'd be great."

She shrugged at me and smiled before looking at the menu. "Thank you."

"I'll take the California burger and some tater tots," Caleb said.

"Me too," Charlie agreed easily, and Stacy marked it down.

Caleb went on to say something about how Lila was ordering for herself and others, but I tuned them out because Charlie turned to look at me. "Good 'ole California burger," Charlie said, shaking his head. "And those… are they tots? I thought they were the round French fries."

"Those are different," Stacy said, overhearing him.

"Those are the fries. Did you want those or the tots?"

"The fries," Charlie said. "Yep, some things never change," he said with a smile, handing her the menu.

He was saying it to be friendly, but I cringed inwardly. It was the second time one of them said it, and while they meant nothing by it, I still took it to heart. Maybe that was a sign that I needed to get out of this town—try something new.

But I loved living on Lake Sutton. I was only thinking I should leave because two hundred pounds of hunk was suddenly sitting on the stool next to me. My judgement was clouded at the moment.

"So, you have a construction company," I said, getting back to the previous subject.

"Yeah, my dad helped me open it a few years ago, and we're doing well… making progress."

"If making progress is what you call selling all of your lots within a month."

Caleb overheard us and leaned over to interject.

"All of your lots, what does that mean?" I asked.

Stacy was down at the other end, talking to Lila, and Charlie sat back on his stool and swiveled to face me. He was the definition of perfection. There wasn't a single thing that I would change about this man's face. He was a man now. He had grown into a man, complete with stubble on his jaw. His straight, square jawline framed his full lips. He was masculine but gorgeous, and I was not prepared for this interaction at all. To say my heart was racing was an understatement.

"I bought some land and we're developing it. I planned the neighborhood, and I sell the lots to individuals with an agreement that I'll be contracting the work on their house. It's going good so far."

"That's amazing," I replied, wishing I had more to say about it. As it stood, I was distracted by seeing them and I knew nothing about construction. I was barely able to keep up with the conversation. He seemed young to be doing something so… amazing. That was the only word I could come up with.

There was a brief pause in our conversation and then Caleb glanced at us like he was about to say something off-topic.

"Lila called them some other name, but it's a soap opera, right? A soap opera is what she's talking about, right? Are you named after a soap opera character?" Caleb stared at me, waiting for the answer.

"Yeah, soaps," I said.

"Why do they call them that?" Caleb asked. "What's that mean, soap opera? What does soap have to do with anything? I've always wondered that."

"I know the answer to this, hang on," Lila said. "I'll tell you guys in just a second but first let me… two more regular cheeseburgers and a basket of fries, and I think that's it. It should be eight burgers that I'm ordering. Ten including theirs."

Stacy looked down to count the number of burgers on her tab, and as we waited to hear the answer, I caught sight of Stacy's dad coming out of the kitchen with my food. I only saw him for a second, and I knew he was headed my way with that bag. He smiled brightly at me, and then his face fell as my eyes widened at him. God bless Stan. He understood my code and he stopped and stood still. I gave him a little shake of my head and shot my eyes toward Charlie who had turned and was listening to Lila. Stan pointed at the kitchen with a questioning look on his face, and I nodded just enough for him to understand that I didn't want my food right then.

I tuned back into the conversation as Lila was still talking about soap operas having to do with ads for actual soaps and detergents since the programs appealed to housewives. I thought it was an interesting piece of information, but it barely sunk into my brain because of the whole exchange I had with Stan and the bag of food. It was hilarious that he actually stopped in his tracks and went back the way he came.

I was smiling when Charlie turned to me again.

"I can't believe you're one of the first faces I see when I come back," he said. "Do you remember when we used to swing on that tire for a whole day at a time?"

"Yes," I answered, feeling thankful that he remembered. "We sang."

He laughed. "We sang so hard. We thought we were rockstars out there."

"We were rockstars," I said.

"I wonder if that tire's still there," he said. "I haven't been back in those woods yet."

"I went out there, but I didn't think to look for the swing," Caleb said.

"You better spray for bugs," Lila said. "That lady who used to come cook, Miss Gabby, remember her? She burned a tick off of me with a match one time."

"She used to plant a bunch of herbs and stuff for bugs," I said. "She had some citronella plants out behind the kitchen. There's a chance some plants are still back there. That stuff's really good for bugs."

"I know the garden you're talking about," Caleb said.

We talked about this for another twenty minutes—about everything—the house, the lake, memories we had from various summers and Christmases. It was good to sit there with them as they reminisced. It made me happy that Eric and I were a part of their childhood memories. They asked about my brother, and I told them the whole story about how he met a girl from Nashville and followed her over there. He had said he was just going to see her for a month or two, and that was nearly a year ago.

"Here's the food," Stacy said, out of nowhere, when she saw her dad come around the corner with all of it. "Oh, yours is here, too, Hope." She looked at me as she handed me my bag. "That took forever to come out," she said, having no idea that I had the exchange with her dad.

It only took a second for her to hand us our food. The tabs were taken care of, and suddenly, our twenty-minute conversation came to a screeching halt as they stood up to leave.

"Hey, you should come by the house sometime," Charlie said. "My wife is in town. I'd love for you to come over and meet her."

He was talking to me, and I smiled and said what I thought was appropriate even though my heart was on the floor.

"Yeah, that'd be great," I said in an unaffected tone.

I felt like a fool. For the last twenty minutes, I had been making plans in my head about how I was going to be the next Mrs. Charles Morgan, and that was the furthest thing from Charlie's mind. He was actually thinking about his own Mrs. Morgan. I felt blood rush to my cheeks, and I set myself in motion, searching for my keys to distract from the fact that I was now in the process of blushing.

In those seconds, I thought back to our conversation this last little while. We sat next to each other and we shared cordial conversation, but he never led me on. The attraction was one-sided and I felt like a total fool.

"I would love to," I said. "I will come see you guys at the house sometime for sure."

I was already planning on heading to the bathroom.

"How long are you in town?" Stacy asked.

"Savannah and I are going to be here for two weeks. Caleb only gets a week. Dad and Casey—who knows with them. They might be here a month."

"Beck's going to be here all summer, too," Lila added.

"We missed it over here," Charlie said. "It's good to be back."

I smiled and acted happy as we said goodbye. I left my bag of food at the bar and told Stacy I needed to go use the restroom.

Chapter 3

Stacy was standing at the bar when I finished my trip to the ladies' room. She stared at me with a neutral but unreadable expression as I approached.

"What?" I asked as she continued to stare.

"You okay?"

"Yeah, what do you mean?" I asked.

"Charlie's married. Who knew. That's crazy."

"Was that more of the Morgan boys?" Stacy's mom, Bridgette, came in just then, and it was the first thing she asked us when she made it in the door.

"Yes," Stacy said.

Stan heard them and came out of the kitchen. "I tried to take Hope's sandwich to her, and she gave me a death stare, so I kept it back in the kitchen with me so she could talk to those boys."

"I didn't give you a death stare," I said, laughing and defending myself.

"The older one, Charlie, he's married," Stacy said, informing her parents.

"Was that his wife with them?" Bridgette asked.

"No, that's Lila," I said. "Donnie's daughter, from Houston."

"Oh, Lila and Beck?"

"Yeah, but Beck wasn't with them," Stacy said to her mom. "Those were two of the Florida boys. Charlie, the oldest one, got married. I looked that woman up while you were in the restroom. Savannah Morgan."

My head whipped around to look at Stacy when she said that. "You looked her up?" I asked.

She nodded. "She's all plastic looking. You don't want to see it."

"Plastic looking?" Bridgette asked. "What's that mean?"

"All perfect and made up," Stacy said.

She was being nice. She was trying to tell me not to look at it or worry about it, but I knew I would do both of those things. Or maybe I wouldn't. I didn't know what I would do. It didn't matter. Charlie Morgan was married, and it wasn't a big deal.

"She's sad about it." I heard Stacy make the statement to her mom. Her careful tone made me believe they were concerned for me. I looked up at them with a smile.

"I don't care if Charlie Morgan got married," I said easily. "I assumed he was, after all this time. A lot of people my age are married."

"Someday you'll just give up and marry Landon," Stacy said.

"Marrying Landon is not giving up," Bridgette said.

"I know it's not," Stacy said. "But Hope could be with Landon any time she wanted, so I think in her mind she'd be settling."

"No, it's not like that," I said. I stood up with the bag of food in hand. "Landon's my brother's best friend. He's my friend. We're just friends."

"They spend three nights a week together," Stacy said.

"Don't say it like that," I said. "It sounds like you're saying we spend the night together. We hang out during the evening hours sometimes. He's really into rock climbing. He's got a whole big wall at his house. He built the whole thing. It's going up the outside of his parents' garage. We spend a lot of time together because I go over there and use his climbing stuff."

There was nothing going on between Landon and me, but it made me feel good that Stacy brought it up. It was a welcome distraction when I was flustered about having a crush on someone who was taken. *How had I not looked for a wedding ring?* That was the furthest thing from my mind. It hadn't crossed my mind during the entire exchange with Charlie. I actually thought I had a chance with him. It was so funny that one person could be having all sorts of thoughts and feelings while the other person was completely oblivious, innocent, and not thinking about love, marriage, and happily ever afters at all.

I liked Charlie so much back in the day, and all those feelings had come back to me the instant I saw him. It was impossible not to like him. He was irresistible, and it wasn't just his looks. His looks were amazing, but that wasn't the only good thing about him. His demeanor and sense of humor were what drew people to him. He was laid back but still comfortable being the center of attention. It was no surprise to me that he had opened a business of his own.

He and Caleb were the conservative-looking ones in the family with shorter hair and practical taste in clothing, whereas Casey had taken after their dad, Max, who had a slightly edgier look and vibe. At least that was how it was when they used to come here.

I knew I shouldn't let myself speculate about the Morgans. There was no hope for a future for Charlie and me, so I just turned it off—I turned off my desire for him like there was a switch.

"I just have these warm fuzzy memories of that family," I said, being honest since Stacy's family seemed so curious. "So many of my childhood summers were spent with them. I love living on Lake Sutton, mostly because I grew up spending so much time out there on the west banks. I loved having my dad work over there."

"Doulos," Bridgette said.

"Do what?"

She pronounced the word again. "Dou-los."

But it was foreign to me, and I shrugged. "What's that?"

"It's the Greek word for slave or servant. It's from the Bible. I'm sure it's from other places, too, but the Bible is where I know it from."

I knew Bridgette Rhodes was a big-time Christian, so it didn't surprise me to hear her come out with the Greek lesson.

"The apostle Paul," she continued, putting her things behind the counter. "He wrote a lot of letters in the New Testament. He calls himself a doulos when he introduces himself, which is the Greek word for bondslave—bondservant."

"Did you just get back from church or something?" Stan asked, poised to head back to the kitchen.

"No, I went to the store. Why?"

"Because what's that have to do with anything?" he asked, looking genuinely curious.

I was so distracted that I hadn't even realized that her comment didn't have to do with anything. I stood there with Stacy and Stan, looking at Bridgette. She pointed at me.

"Hope was saying she had warm fuzzies about the Morgans, and I was thinking about her dad working for them. That was the whole point of the word Paul used to describe himself. There were deals back then where people would work off debts to each other by serving as a slave in a household for a certain period of time, depending on what they owed. And sometimes, even when the debt was paid off, the person would choose to stay and continue to work as a servant in that house because their life was better there than it was before they got there. Paul calls himself doulos to say that he's serving Christ by choice—that his life is better as a slave to the cause of the kingdom." She shrugged. "I was thinking about your dad. He'd probably go back to working over there if the job opened up."

I nodded. Their family loved me and my family, and she meant no offense. "I'm sure he would. I don't think they're hiring anybody, though. We were just talking to Charlie and them about the house, and he said they haven't decided what they're going to do with it yet. They might just sell it."

"They said that at first," Stacy said. "But then they started reminiscing and talking about all the good times they had there."

"I bet they could get two or three million for that place," Stan said. "Even in the shape it's in."

"Mister Donnie said it's being remodeled," Stacy said.

Her dad shook his head. "Well, then I'm sure it's worth more than that."

I held up my bag with one hand as I smiled at the three of them. "Thank you so much for dinner."

"I put some chocolate cake in there for you," Stan said.

"Thank you."

"What are you doing this weekend?" Stacy asked.

I widened my eyes and made a silly, stiff face. "Probably rock climbing," I said, making her laugh. "I'll call you tomorrow or Saturday," I added, smiling.

Stacy walked toward the door with me while her parents stayed in the restaurant. I waved at them one more time on my way out.

"It's insane seeing those guys, huh?"

"Yeah, I mean, kind of," I said with a casual shrug.

"Why are you being aloof."

"Why would I be anything but aloof?"

"I don't know. You should be happy. It's cool that a bunch of good-looking men are coming to Lake Sutton this summer. Charlie might be the only one who's married."

She raised her eyebrows, and I smiled and rolled my eyes at her, shaking my head. "There are guys all over this lake in the summer," I said.

"Those Morgans are some pretty top-notch hunks of beef, though, am I right?" she said, lifting her eyebrows again. "I had forgotten about that family. And then we get two groups in one day. The guys who came in earlier looked good just like these, and I don't think they were married. None of them said they were." She had a faraway look in her eyes as she fanned herself. Stacy had been boy crazy since I'd known her, and I could see her wheels turning about the Morgans.

"Yeah, I can't believe they're here, either," I said. "I wonder if they'll sell the house or keep it."

"I don't know," she said. "But I'm sure we'll see them again this summer."

Chapter 4

I was over at Landon's house the following evening when I got a phone call from my dad. He always called instead of texting, so it wasn't a surprise when my phone rang and I saw his name flash across my screen.

I couldn't answer it. My hands were full of chalk and I was getting ready to start climbing Landon's rock wall, so I didn't pick it up. I told Landon it was my dad and that I'd call him back. Usually, my dad would leave a message and I would hear the signal indicating that I had a voicemail. But today, he called back a second time. I was just about to start climbing as my phone rang again. I quickly wiped off my hands and jogged over to it.

"Hey, what's up?" I said, feeling worried as I pressed the button and put the phone to my ear.

"You'll never believe what happened to me just now," Dad said.

"I have no idea," I said. "Are you okay?" I shrugged at Landon who was looking at me like he was wondering what my dad was saying. My dad sounded lighthearted which wasn't what I was expecting seeing as how he double-called.

"Max Morgan called me and asked me if I wanted a job."

"What? Really?"

"Yes. It's a contract for a year's work, and I get to live out there on the property again. Can you believe that?"

"Are you taking it?"

"Am I taking it? What do you mean? I already took it."

"You told them you would?"

"Yes, of course."

"Do you have to quit your other job?"

"Of course. But it's as much as I'm making at Ace, and I get free rent back in Broken Arrow. They've got that house all fixed up."

"Only for a year, though. You've been at the hardware store for five years. You're managing."

"Yeah, I know, but it's still worth the gamble, Hope. It's Broken Arrow. Even if it only works out for a year, I still want to do it. Plus, he said they may hang onto the house and extend my contract. Max and his boys are talking about buying it."

"And they would be able to afford to have you live there and work there? What kind of people can afford to just hire a man to work and live at their house that they barely ever use?"

"I thought you would be excited," he said. "I thought you would be happy for me."

"Do you feel like you're a servant to them?"

"I guess, if you want to look at it that way. But I don't mind. It's a fulfilling job. It's a beautiful property. I thought you'd remember it."

"I know, I do, and I am happy for you if you're happy, I just thought maybe you were better off where you were. What if they don't need you in a year, and you have to move all your stuff back into an apartment?"

"Well, then I guess I'll have to move my stuff," my dad said.

Landon, who was listening to our one-sided conversation, made a questioning face at me, and I put a finger in the air at him.

"That's really good news," I said happily to my dad since I knew that's what he wanted to hear. "It's awesome."

"Max said you should come by with me."

"He said that?" I asked.

"Yeah, he asked about you and Eric. He said his boys ran into you at Stan's restaurant."

"Yeah, they were there yesterday getting a bunch of hamburgers. It's weird having them back. When are you moving in?"

"Tomorrow. Whenever I want. They're ready for me to start working. I told them I was going to give Ace my two-week's notice. I'm on a month-by-month lease with my apartment, so I'm just going to end it next month."

"Wow, Dad," I said. "I'm happy for you. I think you'll be happy."

"Oh, I know I will. I can't wait to go back to work for the Morgans."

I paused for a minute, thinking about running into them the day before. I had been smitten the whole time I talked to Charlie, and I felt a wave of embarrassment at the thought.

"Congratulations," I said, sounding upbeat.

"Thank you. I'm happy about it."

***

Landon came with me to my dad's apartment later that weekend. My dad had asked me to bring Landon with me so that he could do some heavy lifting and help us make a trip over to Broken Arrow with his things. My dad had a friend with us, too. One of his buddies from work came to help us out with a truck and trailer. His apartment was a small two-bedroom, but he had been in there for a few years and had accumulated quite a few things.

I ran to the store to get some last-minute boxes while the guys packed some of his furniture into the trailer. My errand only took a few minutes, and when I returned, they were loading it up. I spoke to them as I walked toward the apartment with a stack of boxes.

"Do you need help?" Dad asked.

"I should be asking you that," I said, since they were the ones carrying a table. I set the boxes down and stood next to the trailer, balancing the boxes on their side."

"We've got it," my dad said. "How did it go at Ace?"

"Good. The boxes were free—you had plenty that were broken down ready to go, but I had to listen to Carl talk my ear off for about five minutes."

Dad laughed. "Good thing you got away with just five. I bet he told you all about that deck he's building."

"Yes, I know about the deck. I even know what he had for dinner last night." I made the statement as I picked up the boxes to head inside.

"Pot roast?" Dad guessed.

"Salad," I said. "Some kind of salad with a rotisserie chicken."

"Are you talking about dinner already?" Landon asked as he appeared in the doorway carrying two chairs.

I smiled at him and shook my head. "No, I had to hear a whole story from Carl at my dad's work when I went to pick up these boxes. He told me half of his life."

"Because you're Hope Jones and you're too nice," Landon said.

We switched places on the sidewalk since I was headed inside and he was headed out. "It's partly true that I'm too nice, but I was being short with him today. Everyone gets stuck talking to Carl."

"Did you get tape?" Landon asked.

I turned and nodded at him from over my shoulder as I went inside.

I put together boxes and packaged some of my dad's kitchen stuff before moving to a closet in the hall where he had stored a bunch of sheets and blankets.

We were there for two hours, working to pack and get everything into the trailer before we took it to Broken Arrow. The two cities were on the same lake, but they were over thirty miles apart, using the back roads that circled the lake. I knew the roads well. It was a trip I had taken countless times as a child. I'd gone back and forth from Broken Arrow to Graham Springs hundreds of times, and while I took a boat sometimes, most of those trips had happened by vehicle. These roads were slightly different since time had passed, but they were still familiar to me.

"I'm just taking in how everything is changed." I made the statement to Landon as I sat in his passenger's seat. He was driving his car behind my dad on our way to the Morgan's property.

"Have you seen the house at all?" he asked.

I nodded. "I've taken my dad's boat over there a few times. There's a trail through the woods and a swing."

"Is the swing still there?" Landon asked.

I nodded.

"When do you go over there?"

I shrugged. "It's been a while. And, even then, it wasn't all the time or anything. Just whenever I felt like it. I've always liked going into the woods, and I knew no one was on that property."

"I know you like being in the woods. You and Eric used to beg me to go down that trail by Gavin Woodall's yard, and I was scared out of my mind."

"Those woods are not haunted," I said, laughing and rolling my eyes at Landon for bringing up the old urban legend.

"I've never been over here, so I don't know where we're going. I'm not even sure that I've seen the house from the lake. I should have looked at a map."

"You turn at Broken Arrow if you're coming this way, but if you're out on the lake, it's on the south shore right past Sweetbriar Marina. You see the Sweetbriar campground, then the marina, then you go another mile or so and hit the Morgans' property."

"Do you take Paul's little boat all the way over there? I'm surprised you don't run out of gas."

"My dad has a gas can, and I stop at the marina."

"It must be a nice place for you to go hang out over there by yourself. Your dad seems excited about going back."

I hadn't been alone most of the time when I went over there. A couple of times, I had brought girls, and a time or two, I brought a guy. I didn't mention it to Landon because I didn't want to hurt his feelings since I had never invited him. He and I had only gotten closer in recent months since my brother left town.

"He is excited," I said. "I didn't realize how happy he was until I heard him singing out loud."

"I know, he was singing Rolling Stones."

I smiled and shook my head at the thought. "I think Otis Redding sings that song, too," I said.

"Yeah, but he was singing the Stones version," Landon said, smiling at me from over the console.

"Turn right at the light," I said, seeing the road that led to Broken Arrow.

It was only moments later when we pulled up at the property. We went straight to my dad's house, which I hadn't seen in years, and began moving things into it. One of the first things my dad unpacked was a radio, and he tuned it to a classic rock station that we listened to while we made trips from the trailer to the small house. It was about the same size as his last apartment, but it was nicer and newer in spite of having been vacant for the past eight years.

The yard was all worth it. It was amazing with lush woods. I couldn't see the main house or the lake without walking, but I could see a slide and two rope swings at the lake access point. I could also see the edge of the back patio which led to the swimming pool that had been occupied by hoodlums one summer. I took a deep breath.

The Morgan house was one of the nicest properties on the lake. I heard my dad say he thought they could get six or seven million dollars for it now if they decide to sell it. I couldn't blame my dad for wanting to live there. It was serene and peaceful, and

I wore an absentminded smile as I thought of different memories I made there as a child.

I looked up to see Casey Morgan approaching. He was driving a golf cart with a woman riding on the passenger's side. They were an adorable-looking couple. Casey had long hair that he pulled back into a man bun. He was really handsome but with a nonchalant surfer vibe, and the woman in the golf cart with him matched him perfectly. She had on denim shorts and a bikini top.

He parked in the distance, and I watched her get out. Her stomach was so trim that it made me suck in my gut just to look at her. She had long, dirty blonde hair with just enough beach waves that I thought there might be a few dreadlocks. She was like a mermaid. I could tell just by looking at her that she was a free spirit, and I meant that in the most beautiful way. Casey's girlfriend was gorgeous.

My dad and the guys were still loading boxes into the garage, and I had come to carry a box into the kitchen. I was the only one who could see Casey and his girlfriend pull up from the back, so I headed out there to meet them. Casey told her something and then he turned and put his phone to his ear. He stayed back near the golf cart while she headed into the house.

She was carrying a duffel bag and heading toward me like she knew where she was going. I opened the door just as she approached, and I watched as her face fell.

"Oh, hello, who are you?" she asked in a surprised tone, looking around as if searching for clues. She was confused but still friendly. I liked her instantly.

"I'm Paul's daughter," I said. "Were you coming to bring something to my dad?"

"Who?" she asked.

"My dad. Paul Jones. He's the one moving in. He's working here. I'm just here helping him move in."

"Oh, I'm..." she trailed off and looked all around. "I'm sorry, I thought we... me and my husband are staying in the guest house. His family owns this place. I don't know what I'm doing here. It's more like a campus. I feel like I'm at Disneyland."

I glanced at Casey who was still standing at the golf cart, talking on the phone and acting oblivious to his wife.

"There are two other guest houses," I said, hoping this was a misunderstanding. "And I think Mister Max knew my dad was moving into this one today."

"Oh, no, no, I believe you. I'm sure it's my fault. Casey wasn't sure where to take me, and I saw this little house when we pulled up and thought it was the right place."

"There are two other guest houses on the far side of the swimming pool. My guess is they'd have you in there. You're welcome to call Mister Max or ask

Casey, though, just in case there's been a misunderstanding."

"No, I'm sure you're right. I didn't know where to go. I just guessed at this one."

She shrugged the bag onto her shoulder again. She was sweet and I liked her instantly. She was beautiful, too. She had big eyes and pouty lips and her face looked like she had work done even though she hadn't. She naturally looked the way girls tried to look when they had surgery or injections.

"I'm sure you'll love the guest houses," I assured her. "They're furnished and they're really nice. I thought Casey would have known that's where y'all were staying."

She shrugged easily and turned around. "He just brought me out here because I asked him to. He has no idea what's going on. He's busy on the phone with something for his work." She waved at me. "Sorry to bother you."

"No, it's no bother. It's nice to meet you. My dad works here. He worked here for years before when Don and Naomi lived here, and we're just moving him back in."

"Oh, okay, cool. What's your dad's name?"

"Paul," I said. "Paul Jones."

"And you are?"

"Hope," I answered.

"Hope Jones?"

I nodded and smiled at her.

"I'm Savannah. I'm Charlie's wife." She was smiling at me when she said it and I was so transfixed that I didn't understand at first.

"You're Ch-charlie's wife? I thought you were Casey's wife. You look like Casey."

She laughed out loud when I said that. "You're not the first person who has told us that. Me and Charlie are opposites attract, I guess." She shrugged. "He constructs buildings and I jump off of them."

"You jump off of buildings?" I asked, looking stunned.

She grinned at me and shrugged. "Not usually. But I do jump off of things—other things, cliffs and bridges and stuff."

My eyes widened, and she put her hand out to calm me down.

"I use a parachute, though, and it's all really safe."

"Really safe?" I asked with comical hesitancy, causing her to smile.

"It's a calculated risk."

"Are you an adrenaline junkie?" I asked.

She nodded at me without smiling. "That's a complete understatement." Her face broke into a grin and she waved at me as she continued walking back toward Casey.

"It was nice to meet you, Hope Jones."

"Nice meeting you, too," I said.

Chapter 5

One week later

This would be the fourth time this week that I would visit my dad at the Morgans'. The first three times, it was to help my dad move and unpack, but this time, I was making a trip to deliver lunch from Stacy's Black Skillet restaurant.

I had called my dad that morning to let him know I was coming by to bring him a housewarming gift. It was 10am when I called, and I asked if he wanted me to bring him lunch. AJ and Beau, (the Cameron brothers) were nearby when we talked to my dad, and they requested some food. I offered to take orders for the family, and there I was, fourteen burgers and some sides later.

Stacy's dad gave me a discount, and I got all of the food for a hundred dollars, which would show up on my tab later. I had always hated dealing with money, though, and I figured I might end up eating the cost to avoid awkward situations where I'm trying to get money from each of the family members.

It didn't matter. I was only thinking about money because I was trying to calm my nerves and distract myself from the fact that I was going into the main house and everyone would be waiting for me when I got there.

Stacy's parents wanted to impress the Morgans, so they packed everything carefully in an insulated bag. It was all in one big bag and it was cumbersome and heavy, but I smiled and tried my best to seem like it wasn't a struggle as I carried it inside.

They all made various comments when I came in, and I couldn't hear any of them until I made eye contact with Savannah. She was cool and easy, and both of us smiled when we saw each other.

"I didn't try this place the other day when the boys got it," she said.

"Oh, you didn't? You didn't get one of those burgers?"

She was smiling and shaking her head at me as Charlie stepped around her, reaching for the bag. I handed Charlie the bag reluctantly.

"Mine is in there," I said. "Mine and Dad's. I'll grab them really quick and get out of your hair. I'll come get the bag later."

"Stay and eat with us," Savannah said.

"Aw, thank you, but I told my dad I'd meet him at his place. I think we're eating over there."

"Your dad's here with my dad," Charlie said. "No pressure, but you could both just eat while you're here, if you want. What do we owe you for this? Did my dad already pay for it?"

He took the bag and carried it toward the kitchen.

"Yeah, I actually didn't have to… it sounds bad, but I have a running tab at that restaurant, and I haven't paid for it yet."

I wasn't expecting to encounter the Morgans and Camerons on such a grand scale. Some of the family hadn't been here at first, but now it seemed as if they had all converged in the large, two-room area. I had been here earlier in the week and seen most of them, but not all at the same time like this. I saw aunts and uncles and what seemed to be a couple of extra young women besides Savannah.

I glanced around at everyone as they came toward the kitchen, curiously inspecting the container of food. I heard them all remark as they spoke to each other, saying things like "It's from that burger place in Graham Springs."

Charlie set the bag on the table and opened it.

"Mine and Dad's are on the top, and the rest of them are labeled individually," I said.

There was a bag marked, "Hope," and I pointed to it, so Savannah reached in and handed it to me.

"Hey, Paul," Charlie said when my dad came into the room. "We told Hope you should hang out here and eat with us. The food's already this cold, so I thought you'd want to eat as soon as you can."

"It's actually not that cold," I said, touching the bag and feeling how warm it was.

"Up to you," Charlie said. He gave me a hopeful expression, and I smiled and shrugged.

"I definitely don't mind eating here," I said. "I'm hungry."

Charlie and Savannah both gave me a satisfied nod and everybody started gathering around while Max and Donnie set out plates, silverware, and napkins. People got in line to find their orders, so Dad and I got out of their way. We found a spot in the dining room near Astrid and Danny Cameron. Beau was in there as well, but he left to get his own food. While he was gone, Charlie and Savannah came to sit at the table with us.

"Hope, what do you do for a living?" Astrid asked.

I had never thought of myself as having a career, but I told her what my job was. "I work at a pediatrician's office. I do a lot there, but mostly I work in the front—scheduling, billing, and things like that."

"So, I guess you're off on Saturdays," she said.

"Most of them," I said, nodding. "We're open on Saturdays until noon, but we use a skeleton crew and I only have to do it about once a month."

"I thought you might work at the burger place," Astrid said. "We wouldn't have asked you to deliver this all the way out here to us."

"Oh no, I was coming out here to see my dad, anyway. It was no problem."

"Thank you," Astrid said, standing up to get her burger. "Just tell me how much I owe you."

"Oh, it's not, I'm sure it's… it's really not that much."

I was incapable of coolly asking people to pay me back for things.

"Yeah what do we owe you?" Donnie said.

"I think it was… I'll look at the receipt later. I'm not sure exactly. I was just telling everyone else about how I had a running tab over there at the Black Skillet."

"Well, thank you for picking it up," Max said. "Let me know how much we owe you for all this before you leave."

"Yes sir," I said smiling and nodding at Charlie's dad. He wore a ponytail and looked so much like Casey.

"I heard you do some rock climbing," Charlie said to me.

"Where did you hear that?"

He smiled. "Your dad."

"Oh, yeah," I said. "I don't climb many actual rocks, but yes, my friend has a rock climbing wall that he built, and I like using it with him. It really tore my hands up at first. I had blisters from trying to hang on."

I was in the middle of saying this when I realized that Charlie's wife was probably a well-seasoned rock climber. I got lost in that train of thought, and I felt embarrassed and just sort of trailed off.

"But you probably know all about that," I added, looking at Savannah. "Do you do rock climbing?"

"A little bit, but you're probably better at it than I am. I'm out of practice, so my arms would be gassed pretty quick."

"Oh, the arms," I said, shaking my head.

"If Savannah ever climbed a cliff, she'd just turn around and jump off of it," Beau said, chiming in.

"I remember you telling me you like to jump off of things," I said.

"Yep. That's how I met Charlie. Well, not how I met him. But I was down in Miami, jumping with a group of friends."

"Jumping off of a bridge…" Max said.

"I wasn't jumping when we met, but I was in Miami for a jump and I met Charlie at my hotel."

"I thought it was a restaurant," Astrid said.

"A restaurant in my hotel," Savannah clarified.

"Tell them about that time you got arrested," Caleb said.

Caleb was in some sort of law enforcement. I was almost certain he was with the FBI, but it was a known thing—a regular job at his local FBI branch. As far as I knew, he was part of governmental law enforcement, but he wasn't secretive about it. My dad was the one who told me that, and he knew more. Either way, it didn't surprise me when Caleb brought up Savannah getting arrested.

She laughed and shook her head as if recalling the story. "Well, I'm a BASE jumper, so you would think that I got arrested trying to jump from a structure that was illegal to jump from. That's how most of us get arrested. But that wasn't how it happened. I got arrested skydiving, actually. I landed on private property, and the owners pressed charges. I think they were drug dealers."

"If they were drug dealers, they wouldn't get the cops involved," Caleb said.

Savannah shrugged. "Either way, I got off with a warning, but I got arrested and taken down to the station and everything."

"Did you quit all that since you got married?" Astrid asked.

"Hardly," Charlie said. "She's leaving in two months to go to Europe."

"It's a trip of a lifetime," Savannah said, looking a little apologetic. "Charlie's amazing for letting me go. One of my old jumping buddies planned it, and he called and gave me the itinerary—asked if I wanted to go with them. There's four of us." She smiled and let out a contented sigh. "There are sooo many good, legal, amazing places to jump in Europe. I've been to England and France, but he's got us going all over the place—Spain, Germany, Greece, and Norway."

"I've never been out of the country," I said.

"Oh, I love traveling. Though, it's maybe not as glamorous as it looks on internet videos. We travel cheap. I've been on trips with Gavin before, and we stay anywhere and sleep on couches. I'm a low-maintenance companion, and he knows that. I'm the only female going."

Charlie got several looks at that statement, and Savannah leaned over and hugged him. "Charlie knows where he stands with me," she said. She looked at the side of his face with an adoring expression and touched his cheek. "This man has nothing to worry about." She was so certain and convinced that we all believed her.

"In other good news," Max said, hearing Savannah and making an announcement of his own. "We're keeping the house." A few scattered claps and whoops of excitement happened. "We'll have a schedule posted online, so we know who's staying when. Do not forget to check the calendar if you're going to try to plan a trip here. Astrid wanted me to make sure you all knew that you needed to check the calendar." He gestured to my dad. "Mr. Paul is going to be here full-time, so call him if you need anything when you come stay. His number is on the fridge."

A few more people responded with sounds of excitement and my dad smiled and gave a humble nod. The giant dining room table was filling up by the second, and I tried to blend into the background.

"Paul's going to have plenty to do around here, so when you come, leave everything like you found it. Astrid and Danny wanted to keep the house in the family, so they sold it to me and my boys at a very fair price. And family is family, so you're all welcome here any time. We have plenty of room so just *check the calendar* if you want to use it. Oh, and

I might build another structure, an office in the woods. That'll be off-limits if you stumble across it."

"Telling us it's off-limits just makes us all want to go in," Caleb said, causing everyone to laugh.

Max shook his head and smiled because he knew no one would snoop. Max Morgan had everything under control. He had been single for a long time, and he and all three of his sons all had a powerful, mysterious air about them. It was odd to me that he was making all of these announcements in my presence. Part of me thought he forgot I was there, but I knew that wasn't the truth. He was sharp. They all were. I felt like the people in this room could outwit most of the other people in the world.

After Max spoke, people began eating and talking in small groups. He was close enough to me that I could hear continued conversation and I knew that people were asking him questions about the property.

Savannah was sitting in the chair next to me, and she leaned over to speak to me where no one else could hear us. "Would you ever go out with AJ?"

"What?" I asked, whispering and gawking at her.

Her eyes widened just a little. "I think AJ is planning on asking you out. What would you say if he did?"

"AJ is a player," I said.

She gave a little shrug and smile. "Some girls like a lady's man."

Our exchange was extremely discreet. We were speaking patiently and whispering where we could barely hear each other.

"And besides, you can just go out with him one time. He's a nice guy. You guys could probably hang out with Charlie and me."

"How do you even know he wants to ask me out?" I asked.

I felt silly for asking, but the whole interaction was unexpected, and I waited for her answer.

She hesitated. The conversation next to us had grown quiet, and she didn't want to be obvious.

"He told me," she said, finally, with an easy shrug.

The whole situation made me smile. It was a nervous smile, but I was smiling nonetheless. Savannah glanced at me.

"You're smiling. Do you want him to ask you?"

"I'm not smiling because of that. I'm just nervous. I didn't expect you to say any of this."

"Tots?" Danny, Astrid's husband was holding a basket of tots from over my shoulder, offering it to Savannah and me.

"No thanks," she said, shaking her head. I reached out and took a few, thanking him. I was happy that he bailed me out of an unexpected conversation.

AJ Cameron was extremely desirable—one of the more charismatic of the grandkids—and he was angelic-looking to boot. He had a reputation for being a player. I was well aware that I had no long-term dating potential with AJ, but I couldn't help but be a little flattered that he mentioned me.

Chapter 6

Eight months later

Spring was knocking at our door. I could feel it in the air. The temperature was in the high fifties today, which was too cool for some people, but I thought it was glorious outside, and I wanted to get outdoors.

I got up early and went out to Broken Arrow to see my dad. I was in a great mood. It was Saturday morning, and I had the weekend off. The sky was clear, and the air was crisp, and I couldn't wait to go to the Morgans' and get outside.

It had been a few weeks since I had seen my dad, and I told him I would come by and visit and then eat some lunch.

He called when I was on my way out there, saying that he was at the main house. I was planning on making lunch at his house, and I had some groceries with me that I brought in a cooler. I told him I would stop and put the groceries away first, which I did.

I left my car at his house and walked across a few acres to the mansion where I saw my dad's truck along with a few other vehicles—some from a security company.

I went in through the side entrance since I could see some action in that area. My dad was talking to the guys from the security place, and he smiled and started toward me as soon as he noticed me. The other guys continued talking as Dad started coming my direction.

"Hey baby, you look beautiful."

"Is everything okay?" I asked, looking at the guys.

"Oh, yeah definitely. We've just been having some problems with the alarm, and they came by to check it out." He glanced at the guys. "I'm going to be a minute over here," he said, reluctantly. "They were scheduled to come yesterday, and they couldn't make it, so I need to stay here and explain this to them. It might be an hour or so."

"That's fine," I said with a nod. "I wanted to get outside. I might go fishing or out to the swing. I can meet you back at your place in a little while for lunch."

"Sounds good," my dad said, nodding. "Are you staying for lunch?"

I nodded. "I brought food. I already took everything over to your house."

"Okay, great, thank you. Do you want me to just call you when I'm done here?"

"Yeah, let me know when you're finished, and I can meet you back at your house."

My dad nodded, and I smiled and barely glanced at the guys who were still standing nearby, half-listening to our conversation. I walked away, going the way I came and they joked with my father about how nice it was to have a daughter that brought him lunch on the job. I pretended not to hear them since they hadn't meant for me to.

I enjoyed walking in these woods, so I took my time, looking around and breathing the crisp air. It was as if spring desperately wanted to come, but the last edge of winter still hung in the air. There were a few clouds in the sky, and the sun was peering through them. I had a clear view of the lake for a while, but then I lost sight of it as I headed back toward my dad's cottage. I hadn't been out here in a while, and I smiled at some of the familiar sights and sounds.

I came to a trailhead, and rather than continue walking toward my dad's place, I took the trail. I hung a right and continued walking into the woods, toward the opening where I would eventually find the tire swing. The trail had been overgrown last year when my dad first started back, but they had crews come in and clear it again since then. I looked all around, taking in the woods.

This trail was familiar, and I felt at home and relaxed as I stared at the trees and ferns. I couldn't help but think of Charlie as I walked. It was a place we used to go to all the time.

My heart ached for him, and I wondered what he was doing now. Savannah had passed away tragically. It had happened last fall on that trip to

Europe. My dad told me when it happened, but I hadn't seen or talked to Charlie since then. I had an old phone number for him, but it had been so long since I used it that I had a hunch he had a new number by now.

The Morgans didn't meet in Arkansas that Christmas. They had plans to do it in the future, but there were still renovations and repairs being done around the house, and they decided to wait until the following summer. That was coming up in just a few months, which was why my dad was ironing out all the kinks with the alarm.

Anyway, I hadn't seen Charlie since the incident happened, so I looked it up on the internet to make sure it was the truth. There was an article about it, and some photos, and I felt absolutely gut-wrenched for Charlie.

I had run into a couple of other members of the family since I heard about it, but we never brought up Charlie or his wife. I had no idea what he was doing now.

I thought of him as I walked down the trail, and in my mind, I pictured him as a younger boy, a pre-teen, walking ahead of me, swinging a stick and clearing the woods. He and I talked sometimes, and sometimes we would simply abide in each other's presence, listening to the sounds of the woods like I was doing now.

I heard footsteps, and by the time I looked up, he was only a few feet from me. I yelped in fear and stepped back, holding my hand out and creating distance between myself and the bedraggled man.

"Oh my, what the, what in the… Charlie, is that you? My goodness, Charlie Morgan, you scared the living daylights out of me. What are you doing out here? I was just thinking about you!"

Charlie came in for a shy, brotherly hug, and I hugged him back tentatively.

"I was seriously just thinking about you," I said. "I came to… my dad is at the main house, seeing to some stuff with the alarm. I came out here to hang out with him, but he had to do that, so I told him I was going to the woods. What are you doing out here by yourself?" I asked, looking behind him as if expecting to see Casey or Caleb. "You remind me of Casey," I said.

Charlie laughed at that. "I'm going to tell Casey you think he looks like a homeless man."

I laughed. "You don't look homeless," I said, drawing out the word as I tried to think of a better one to describe him.

He chuckled as he stepped away from me. He looked thin. I took in his lean frame, thinking he had lost a little weight since the last time I saw him.

"You literally screamed out of fear when you saw me, and I wasn't even trying to scare you. I just walked up."

"I did think you were bigfoot at first, but that had nothing to do with how you look."

He laughed, which was what I was hoping for. I reached out and absentmindedly grabbed a branch tearing off a leaf so that I would have something to do with my hands.

I was no longer attracted to Charlie like I used to be, those feelings had turned off the minute I found out he was married. But I still got nervous from running into someone in the woods.

"I'm sure I look terrible," he said. "Which makes it hilarious what you said about Casey."

"Casey's handsome," I said. "Don't you dare tell him I tried to say otherwise."

"It does feel like you were trying to roast him a little bit, comparing him to me in the state I'm in," he said.

I shook my head at him. "You're roasting yourself right now," I said.

Charlie let out an absentminded laugh as he swiped at a branch. "I haven't looked in a mirror in months," he said.

"Why not?" I asked.

I had not planned on pretending to be oblivious. That was just what came out of my mouth in the moment.

"Because my wife died," he said, being brutally honest.

"Yeah, I heard about that," I returned. "And I'm so sorry. I didn't know if I should mention it."

"I bought the ticket," he said.

"What?"

"The ticket. Her ticket. The whole trip. She couldn't have afforded to go without me. I paid for that ticket. I bought it for her."

I glanced at him. "Yeah, but she wanted to go," I said. "It's not like you put a gun to her head. She wanted to go. She was talking about it when I was over here. You can't put that on yourself. What if you bought her a car and she got into an accident while driving it? Would you be blaming yourself for that?"

"Maybe. Probably. I don't know. I haven't thought about that. This is a little different. I surprised her with the trip. She mentioned it to me, but she didn't think she could go, and I surprised her with the ticket."

I stared at him. We were mostly in the shade, but some sunlight filtered through the canopy of trees. I took him in. He didn't seem dirty, but he smelled like he'd been out there working all morning, his clothes were wrinkled, and he hadn't shaved in a long time. The whole thing seemed like Charlie's twin brother, the wild man, who had been out there in the woods.

"Where do you sleep?" I asked at the thought.

"What do you mean, where do I sleep?"

"Where are you staying?" I said, backpedaling. "I mean, where, how long are you staying here? How long have you been in Arkansas?"

He grinned at me. He didn't grow a ton of facial hair, and his beard was patchy, but I stared at the hair that lined his jaw.

"You have a beard," I said.

He rubbed his jaw.

"How long are you in town?" I asked.

"I've been here for five months."

"Five months? What?"

He looked at me like he was surprised at me for being surprised.

"Did you *move* here?"

"Not really. Not officially. I'm just here right now. I'm still working and carrying on with the development in Miami, but I'm doing it remotely. My dad and brothers are still in Florida and they check in on the operation for me."

"Are you just staying here forever? Indefinitely? My dad didn't tell me you lived here now."

"Because I told your dad not to tell anyone," he said. "No one knows I'm here—not even Astrid and Danny and them."

I looked him over. "How do you eat?"

"I get groceries delivered, or I drive down to Little Rock to go shopping. Basically, all I eat is eggs, rice, and avocado, anyway."

"I was thinking you could use a cheeseburger and a chocolate milkshake," I said, joking with him tentatively.

He let out a little laugh but didn't say anything.

"If being here's such a big secret for you, then why are you telling me now?"

"I, uh, don't know, actually. I was out here taking a break, and I heard you coming. I saw you, and it was by instinct that I walked over to you. I didn't even think about it."

"I was about to go to the swing."

"I figured. That's where I was. I replaced that tire with a new one, and I hung a hammock on the same tree."

"Instead of the tire?"

"No, in addition to it."

"How?"

"Well, the tire swing is out on a limb, and I attached the hammock to the other side of the tree trunk. The two don't interfere with each other. Come on. Come see. You'll like it. It's perfect for singing Coldplay to the top of your lungs."

I laughed and followed him down the trail until it gave way to a small opening where I knew I would see the tire swing. It was there, but there were now other things, too. I looked around Charlie, trying to get a better view.

"What is all this?" I asked, taking it in. I saw a large rope hammock like I was expecting, but there was also a deck. There was a rectangular wooden deck in the area adjacent to the tire swing and the hammock.

"Oh, whoa, this is so nice. There's a whole patio over here now. When did y'all have this done?"

"I did it," he said.

"You did it? What do you mean you did it?"

"I built it," he said. "I'm still building it. I've been out here working all morning. I was just taking a break when I heard you."

I scanned the area, taking it all in. "This is professionally done," I said, sounding stunned.

Charlie smiled and nodded a little. "Good, because I'm a professional."

Chapter 7

"I thought you were a contractor," I said. "I thought you were the guy in a suit who planned the building and hired the workers.

"I am, but I do both. My dad had me in building classes when I was old enough to pick up a hammer. He wanted me to become a shipbuilder."

"Oh, my gosh, I totally remember you building a boat that one time," I said. "I'm tying it all together now. I had no idea your dad wanted you to do that."

"Yeah and that's what got me started on building. It's fun. I wasn't even thinking about the property value when I came out here and did this. It's therapeutic. It's fun for me."

I looked him over, scanning his appearance. "Are you living out here?"

He laughed and shoved at my shoulder before turning to walk away—toward the deck. I followed him. "I know I stink, but geez. I suddenly feel compelled to shave and shower since you keep calling me homeless."

"No, I, I just, it's so nice out here. You *could* sleep out here if you wanted."

"I sleep in the guesthouse," he assured me. "But I come out here all the time. I've been out here since about six this morning."

I walked over to the deck and climbed onto it. The entire edge was lined with two steps leading up to a large platform. Half of it was shady and half was in the sun, and I moved to the sunny half and stooped to my knees before turning over and lying down comfortably.

The temperature was cool, and the bright sunlight felt warm and wonderful. I relaxed out there, closing my eyes and letting the sun hit me. I was still lying stretched out on the deck when I felt and heard Charlie come up there with me. I sensed him getting closer and I felt when he got to his knees and then stretched out next to me.

I peeked as he got settled, but I closed my eyes again once I saw that he was planning on lying next to me. We stayed there, basking in the sun, for what must've been twenty or thirty minutes. We said not a word to each other for an incredibly awkward amount of time. At first, I noticed the silence, but then I didn't notice it anymore. The sun shone on our faces and cut through the cool morning air. Our bodies didn't touch.

The whole thing felt like he was my brother. In past years, I would have been having feelings for him, but today Charlie felt like my brother. I wanted to help him, but I didn't know how. He was obviously devastated or he wouldn't be out here, looking like the wild man of Cleburne County. For a while, I didn't know what else to do besides lie out there next to him and not say anything.

"It's not your fault," I said finally.

"I know. Deep down I know."

"Not that I don't like having you in Arkansas, but how long do you plan on staying out here and doing this?"

"Doing what?"

"Doing what you're doing. Being alone," I said.

"I'm being productive," he said. "I'm not anti-social. I talk to people on the phone and take care of emails and other business."

"Have you touched anyone?" I asked.

I reached out and gripped the air until I felt his arm. I took a hold of his forearm and gave it a squeeze. I heard him take a deep breath, and I sat up and did it again. I gave small, gentle, massage-therapy-type squeezes on his arm from his forearm up to his shoulder.

"How long has it been since you made contact with another human being?" I asked, continuing to touch his arm with the same neutral attention I would give to a big ball of dough. I looked down at him. "You should have a little human interaction."

"I haven't touched another human in so long. But I'm not touchy-feely in my everyday life. Even your dad, I see him, but we don't, he doesn't… we've barely shaken hands since I've been back."

"You should go to Little Rock and get a massage," I said.

Charlie sat up, turning to face me casually. "That's probably not going to happen, honestly."

"Look, face that way," I said, gesturing and telling him to turn around.

"You don't need to…" He shook his head, trying to deny the possibility of a backrub, but he needed some kind of physical contact, and I felt obligated as a human to help him. I wanted the best for Charlie.

"Just face that way for a second," I said. "If Eric were in your shoes, I'd want someone to… just face that way for a second… yep. Thank you. Oh, my goodness, Charlie, you're actually a…" I paused and rubbed his upper back with the edge of my hands, warming him up, trying to break his muscles loose. "You are a solid rock back here, Charlie. You're unbelievably tight. I can't even break through here to get to your… you seriously do need to drive somewhere and get a massage. Or even pay someone to come out here."

"What about you?" he asked, sighing as he slumped his head and shoulders in a relaxed pose.

"I'm not a professional."

"No, not massage. Are you still dating my cousin?"

He was just making conversation.

We were not flirting.

"No one's ever really dating your cousin," I said, talking about AJ.

"I knew you went out with him a time or two last year," he said.

"We hung out a couple of times," I agreed. "Honestly, I'm probably closer to dating this other guy. Goodness, gracious, Charlie, your back. I'm feeling a bad patch of knots right here."

He laughed at the fact that my thumb could not penetrate the solid block of brick on his back.

"How long are you planning on staying here?" I asked.

"Why? It's numb right there."

"It's unbelievably tight." I continued by digging my fingertips into his back, trying to be gentle with him but get some blood flowing to his tight back. "I'm really sorry about what happened, but..." I trailed off because I didn't want my words to come across as insensitive, and I was relatively sure they would.

"But what?" he asked when I didn't continue.

"Nothing. I shouldn't… it's not my place to say anything."

"What were you going to say?" Charlie asked, turning to look at me from over his shoulder.

I had been rubbing his back, but I paused and put my hands down, focusing on his face. "I was just going to say that you're out here with nobody. You're all alone. It's not like you're out here on vacation. You're being a hermit, which is fine if that's what you need to do, but I was just wondering how long you were going to do that because I like you and I want to see good things happen in your life. And even as I say these words, I know they're offensive because I would be offended if someone was saying them to me. You can do whatever you want. It's your house, and your job, and your life in Miami. You can do whatever you want. I was just… I care about you as a person."

"I didn't really see myself as being out here alone. I'm just using the house because I wanted some peace and quiet. I'm also out here making sure the work is getting done that my dad contracted."

"Where are you staying?"

"In the guest house closest to the pool."

"I'm surprised my dad didn't tell me you were here."

"He didn't tell anyone," he said. "I'm just trying to be left alone."

"That's what I'm saying. For how long?" I asked.

"What? Why does that matter?"

"It doesn't. You can do whatever you want. I just wondered if you had a plan."

"Not really."

"Well, regardless of what you choose to do with your time, or what state you choose to live in, you should really try to make yourself understand that what happened is not your fault."

He gave me a little smile that was full of all sorts of emotions. "Thank you," he said quietly.

"I know it's easier said than done, but ultimately you have to figure out a way to make yourself believe it's not your fault. We all have our own path, and Savannah was choosing that path before she met you. God knew all this would happen."

"That is not a fun thought. Let's talk about something else."

"Okay, like what?" I asked.

"Who's the other guy you're cheating on my cousin with?"

"One, I'm not with AJ. We went out a couple of times when he was in town. I don't even talk to him when he's in Chicago. I'm sure he's seeing other people in Chicago. But the guy is a friend. He was my brother's best friend, but then my brother followed a woman to Tennessee, and Landon and I… we didn't really hang out all that much before Eric left, but now that he's gone it's like we sort of needed each other to fill that void. I hang out with him a lot more than your cousin."

"Have you ever kissed him?" he asked.

"Landon? No."

"Have you ever kissed AJ?"

"AJ kissed me."

"You didn't let him?"

"Yeah, I let him. We kissed. But it wasn't a big deal."

"And those are the only two dudes in your life?" he asked. "My cousin who visits sometimes and kissed you, and your brother's best friend who will do in a pinch because you're both lonely?"

"Oh, now you're just messing with me so we forget you stopped talking to people and getting haircuts."

"I talk to people every day, and I don't need a haircut because I… I like my hair like this."

Charlie ran his hand through his hair.

"It's lighter grown out," I said.

"Is it?"

"It's crazy. You look so much more like Casey."

"Yeah, hair changes a lot," Charlie said, still fiddling with his longer locks. It was a little short to pull into a ponytail, but it was long enough to be tucked behind his ears, which was what he did. I watched him do that with one side.

I was proud of myself. Even in Charlie's unkempt state, he was a fine specimen of a man. I could be tempted to take advantage of his fragile mindset and hope for a rebound relationship with him. But I truly didn't see him that way. Things had turned off for me with Charlie when I realized he was married. The whole thing was deadbolted shut when I figured out how much I liked Savannah. I had lost feelings for Charlie back then. He had been in hiding for months, so I could only imagine what he had been through. I could tell by the way he looked at me that the lack of feelings was mutual. We stared at each other with a casual look that was raw and honest—a look of friendship.

"That actually felt amazing, what you did on my back," he said. "Thank you. It's itching where you touched it."

"I'm telling you... you need to make an appointment and drive down to Little Rock. I'll make one for you if you want."

"Do you know somebody specific?"

"No, but I'll look at reviews and ask a few people."

"I'd be open to seeing a masseuse if you find somebody you recommend. If not, I'll just wait until I go back home. I think Caleb has somebody at his chiropractor's office that he uses."

"There he is. Look at you, talking about going back home, and joining the world."

"I don't know," he said, reluctantly. "I don't know what I'm thinking. I just said it to get you off my back."

"I'm not on your back. I'm trying to help your back." I laughed a little and then looked at him. "I'm sorry. I don't mean to pry. You should take as long as you need to do whatever you want. It's your life."

"I understand that I can't hide from the world forever. People will be coming out here during the summer and then again for Christmas. I guess I just had it in my head that I would wait for them this summer and then go back with my dad."

"Then you already had a plan."

"I don't know. I'm not putting myself on a time schedule. I'm making it work remotely with my development. My dad and brothers are helping me out."

"It's none of my business, anyway, Charlie. I just know what a rockstar you are, and I know you can get past this."

"I know," he said after a few seconds of silence. "I just keep going back to all the things again and again. I keep thinking about how she promised me there would never be an accident because of how carefully she always planned and prepared. I think about the fact that I bought the ticket."

"Charlie, you have already told me about buying the ticket several times, and I just started hanging out with you. You bought the ticket. You bought the ticket. You bought it. You bought the ticket. We buy people things—especially people we love. That's what we do. You loved her, and you bought her a nice gift that she really wanted. I was there when she was talking about it. It was her trip and her idea. So what if you bought it? You were married by then, so technically it was your collective money. You have to think of a way to get past it, or you'll be paralyzed from doing anything else with your life. Savannah wouldn't have wanted that. She wouldn't have wanted you still here, six months later, talking about buying that ticket. You bought the ticket. It's a fact, but it's not one that really matters. Are you being arrested? No. You're not in trouble with the law. You didn't make her do anything against her will. It's a fact that you bought it, but it's one that you'll have to get past if you want to be able to live."

"Well, thank you, but I really don't care to right now, so that's something that's going to have to come slow."

"You don't care to live?" I asked, sounding shocked.

"I just don't have any sudden urge to go back to Miami and get back to life as I knew it right this second."

I grinned at him and touched his hand. "Good, because I need somebody to push me on the tire swing."

Chapter 8

Charlie Morgan

Three months later

It was now May, and the renovations on the lake house were complete. The family would start rolling in during the weeks to come. There was never a time during the summer when everyone in the family would be in Arkansas at the exact same time, but the calendar was full during those months with most of the bedrooms and guesthouses being spoken for.

Max had taken over the master bedroom as his own, and even if he wasn't currently in Arkansas, no one stayed in there besides him. He was also building another structure on the property. Plans were made and the construction was scheduled to begin later that summer.

Charlie knew all of this because he had been staying in the guesthouse for almost nine months. He had been on-site, so he was helping his father envision and design the plans for the secret cabin in the woods. It would be small and modest on the outside but expansive and high-tech on the inside with an underground bunker.

Charlie didn't ask his dad any questions about his plans. If you asked Max what he did for a living, he would say that he was a stock trader. That would explain why he seemed to sometimes come into windfalls of money. But there was speculation about Max. He traveled a lot and was an expert in martial arts and weaponry. Casey seemed to follow in Max's footsteps. The two of them both worked in stock trading, and they traveled together quite a bit. Some people speculated that Max and Casey were modern-day pirates, but Caleb had a career in the FBI, and he would know if his own family was doing anything illegal. They did, however, look like modern-day pirates with their man buns, suntans, and leather sandals.

Charlie chose not to worry about what his dad and brother did during their travels.

Max has always been a secretive person and this construction project in the woods was not something Charlie went around talking about—he wasn't tempted to tell anyone. The main person he talked to already knew there would be construction on the property, and she didn't care. She was discreet, and she knew not to tell anyone. Charlie was in the middle of having a conversation with his father, and they were talking about Hope, so Charlie was thinking about her at the moment.

"Hope was saying how it flooded under those trees when we were little, and I looked into it, and she was right. I didn't remember that. I'm glad we moved plans for the project to the other location. I like it better there, anyway."

"How did she remember that?" Max asked.

"I don't know. Her dad didn't even remember it, only Hope did. That's why I went to the zoning office to confirm. She said she remembered looking out at the trees and seeing the water pooling. I think she has a photographic memory or something. When she tells a story, she gives details that make me think she's got some kind of ability to snap pictures in her mind. Her recall ability is amazing. She remembers those kids' charts at her work."

"I knew she was sharp," Max said.

"And I knew something must be going on with you two if she's got you shaving." He pushed at Charlie's shoulder, and Charlie made a face at his dad.

"Hope might have indirectly had something to do with me physically shaving my face, but it's not because I'm trying to impress her."

"Then what'd she say to get you *physically* shaving?" Max asked, teasing him.

"She told me the truth, which was that you guys would all be coming here this weekend. She said it was weird enough that I was living out here by myself and that I should at least shave to avoid a bunch of questions from everyone about my mindset."

"She's right," Max said. "I was about ready to take it to you if I showed up and saw you out here still looking like a bear."

"You look like a bear half the time."

"That's because I am a bear," Max said.

"But you're more of a fox… or a wolf. Dapper and charming and cunning. Last time I saw you, you were looking more like… a sloth?"

"*A sloth*?" Charlie said. "That's a little too far. I haven't stopped working since I've been out here."

"I was talking about looks more than work ethic, but I'm glad you shaved either way," Max said. "It wasn't good to see you out here not looking in a mirror, and I'm glad that girl finally got you doing it."

"I'm not doing it to impress Hope. She just suggested that I do it so you guys don't give me a hard time."

"You already said that," Max said. "And you've mentioned Hope five or six other times since I've been here."

"So?"

"So, it's only been a few hours."

"Well, we hang out quite a bit. I see her all the time, and talk to her, so it's just natural that I bring her up. I wanted to tell you things she said."

"And you have no feelings for her?"

"No, dad, no. Of course not. We're not. Hope and me… we're friends, but nothing more than that. She's friends with this other guy, and AJ is coming out here tomorrow, and I know he's planning on trying to talk to her."

"Uh, never mind," Max said in a turned-off tone.

"What?"

"She's seeing some guy, and she's trying to come over here and talk to AJ. I was mistaken about her. I didn't know she was that type of girl."

"She's not. She's not technically seeing that guy. She's just friends with him. They hang out and do rock climbing and stuff."

"Why are you so upset about it?" Max asked.

"I'm not upset about it."

"You looked upset when you were talking about that guy."

"I didn't mean to look upset," Charlie said shaking his head. "Hope's a friend. We were friends a long time ago, and we picked up where we left off."

"Is she seeing AJ or that other guy?"

"I don't know," Charlie said, feeling annoyed. "If she's seeing either of them, it's AJ, but I don't know. All I know is that he called her to see if she wanted to come over here tomorrow."

"And is she coming?" Max asked.

"Yeah, but she was probably planning on stopping by, anyway."

"Why are you trying to tell me you're not into this girl?" Max asked, pulling back to study his son.

"I'm not into her," Charlie said. "If you haven't noticed, I'm still in the middle of nowhere from everything that happened with Savannah."

"Well, just because you're in the middle of nowhere geographically doesn't mean you're in the middle of nowhere emotionally. I've been able to tell you're doing better, and I know she's the one who caused it."

"I'm not trying to deny that," Charlie said shaking his head.

He and his dad were in the kitchen, and Charlie suddenly sprawled and grabbed onto his dad, holding onto his arm and neck in such a way that he knew he wanted to engage in grappling. Max had done this move with his sons throughout their lives, and he fought back, just enough to engage with Charlie, both of them smiling.

"Oh, now you're trying to wrestle your old man? You're coming in here trying to tell me you're not in love, and then you want to wrestle?"

"I'm not in love," Charlie said, still engaging in a controlled arm and neck hold with his dad. He tossed him away, standing up straight and taking a deep breath.

"Well, you're certainly mentioning Paul's daughter a lot. Casey thought that's why you were still over here. He said you were just going to get married and stay here."

"Neither of y'all know what you're talking about. Hope and I are the furthest thing from dating. You can tell when a woman has feelings for you, and I can just tell that she doesn't. The other day, I made her a burrito, and she scarfed it down in about four bites and then burped really loud." Max laughed and Charlie shook his head, imagining other things Hope had done and said in the last few months. "She's with me all the time, but she is *not* interested. I'm telling you, she talks to me about other guys. She's open with me in a way that I can tell she's not trying to impress me at all."

"Plus, she's probably not smart enough for you," Max said. "I don't remember Paul's daughter being all that bright."

Max was baiting his son, but Charlie didn't even realize it. "What? You just said she was sharp when I told you about the flood. We had the whole conversation about her memory. She's bright. She's plenty bright. Brightness has nothing to do with the reason I'm… she's just… we're just friends."

"Okay," Max said, putting his hands up in surrender. "I won't say any more about it."

"She's not *not* bright, though. Just so you know. She's really smart."

"She's not *not* bright, got it," Max said.

"I just don't want you thinking that because she's really smart. She can remember anything. Eric too. They're both smart people."

Max shook his head, putting his hands into the air again. "Fine," he said. "They're both geniuses. Did Eric ever come back?"

Charlie shook his head. "He's still in Nashville with that girl."

Charlie continued talking to his dad about other things, but his mind kept wandering to Hope. *Did he have feelings for her?* Charlie thought it would be years before he was ready to love again. He thought he might never love again. He didn't think of loving Hope as an option. He didn't even think of loving anyone as an option. But he caught himself going back to her in his thoughts after his dad brought the whole thing up.

He talked to Hope on the phone that night, and he tried not to act any different than usual. She mentioned AJ and the fact that she would be coming over the next day, and Charlie felt a pang of jealousy. He pretended he was completely unaffected. He hated that his dad had put these thoughts into his head. Before today, the thought of being with Hope hadn't even crossed his mind. He was still mourning the loss of Savannah, and moving on wasn't an option. *But was love an option?* Charlie felt like, technically, it might be an option by this point. He was suddenly confused and flustered, and he blamed his father for all of it.

But he talked on the phone with Hope for over an hour that night, and he started to notice how well they got along. He had fun talking to her, and he thought she might have been the difference between him being okay and not being okay during these last few months.

The two of them spoke about their day, and then they talked about food and then about television. It was light and easy conversation, like always. Nothing was fake or forced.

Charlie wondered if he had feelings for Hope Jones. He knew beyond the shadow of a doubt that if he did have any feelings for her, they were not mutual. But he couldn't deny that he felt something. Something had shifted with him.

"What time are you coming over tomorrow?" he asked when they were wrapping up their conversation.

"I planned on coming out there when I get off work," Hope answered. "I think AJ's coming in at noon."

Charlie wondered why she cared so much about when AJ would be there. She had said it herself that she knew there would never be anything long-term with her and AJ. *So why was she even coming out there to hang out with him?*

"Charlie?"

"Yeah?"

"You were quiet for a long time. You were asking when I was coming over tomorrow, and I said after work."

"Okay, that's fine," he said, feeling agitated and confused.

"All right, well, I guess I'll let you go," she said. Her tone was slightly hesitant. It was as if she could tell something was wrong with him.

"Okay, yeah. I'll talk to you tomorrow," he said, trying his best to act normal and say normal things.

"Okay see, you tomorrow. Night, Charlie."

"Night, Hope."

Chapter 9

Hope Jones

The following day

"Are you sure you don't want me to come?" Stacy asked.

"I would, but I don't know what to expect," I said. "It's their get-together. I already feel like I'm intruding going by myself."

"I am so jealous," Stacy said.

"I'm so nervous," I said, hoping to make her feel better. "I'd love if you could go with me."

"I want to so bad."

"I mean, I thought you'd want to be with Charlie, and I could try to talk to AJ this time, but if you're thinking about talking to AJ, I could talk to Charlie. Also, what about Beck or any of the others? Who all's in town?"

She was being hyper, and I shrugged and gestured to the food. "They ordered twenty burgers, that's all I know."

We were outside of the restaurant. I had volunteered to come to pick up some food on the way to Broken Arrow because something went wrong with their plans to barbeque.

"What would make you say that about Charlie?"

"Say what about Charlie? That I wanted to talk to him? Because he's hot."

"No. What would make you say you thought I would want to start seeing Charlie."

"You already are."

"No, we aren't," I said defensively.

She made a face at me.

"We're just hanging out because we're friends. I think he's starting to feel better about his wife. I think he'll be going back to Florida soon."

"He's leaving?" she asked.

I nodded and shrugged. "That's the plan. He'll head back after this summer."

"You're going to be devastated. You hang out like every day."

"I will miss him," I said, not bothering to deny it. "But we don't hang out every day. Twice a week. Three times, max."

She made another face at me.

"Maybe four times."

"And you text all the time," she said.

"Not all the time. You're making something out of nothing."

"I am not," she said, shaking her head.

"Well, I promise there's nothing going on between Charlie and me," I said. I sounded convinced because I was convinced. There was nothing going on between us. "I'm helping him. He went through a lot and I'm helping him. I actually don't feel attracted to him. I don't want somebody who's been married. That's too much baggage for me."

"I see what you mean, but I don't care," she said "I'm totally good with Charlie, baggage or no baggage."

"I don't think he's ready for all that, anyway."

"Scope it out tonight," she said.

I smiled. "I will. I'll let you know who's all at the house."

I closed my trunk and smiled at her.

"You're seriously the luckiest girl in the world," she said. "And you're beautiful," she added rolling her eyes and pretending to be mad. "It's so freaking frustrating." She was clearly joking, and she smiled and reached out to hug me. "You're going to kiss him tonight. Text me later and let me know how it went," she said.

"Kiss who?" I asked. "I'm not thinking about kissing anybody. I'm just going over there to eat."

"Who did you think I was talking about?" she asked.

I shrugged and looked at her with wide eyes. "AJ?"

"Yes," she said. "And it's funny that you didn't know who I meant. You thought I meant Charlie, and I was talking about AJ. You kissed AJ last time he was in town."

"He kissed me," I clarified.

"Are you going to kiss him back if he kisses you again?"

"I have no idea," I said, smiling and shaking my head at her. "I haven't even thought about that. I'm just going over there to deliver their dinner."

"And eat with them," she said.

"And eat with them," I agreed.

I told myself that there was nothing to be nervous about. Technically, there wasn't. I had no real plans with any of them. I was doing them a favor by delivering their food. I felt anxious as I made the forty-minute drive to their property, and I reminded myself that I didn't have to stay and eat if I felt uncomfortable.

I had brought the Morgans food before, and I did the same thing I did last time and carried the large insulated bag to the side door. I knocked, and AJ Cameron was there to let me in.

"Hey, gorgeous," he said, smiling at me. He had light brown hair and ice blue eyes, and it was his destiny in life to be a lady-killer.

"I saw you pull up. Let me take this." AJ reached out for the bag, and I handed it to him. Charlie came into the room just as AJ leaned in to take the bag, and I performed an awkward hug as I gave him the burgers.

He looked different—Charlie did. He had cut his hair and shaved, and I hadn't been expecting that. My heart raced a little at the sight of the old Charlie.

"Burgers," I said, talking to both of them and trying not to get tripped up on Charlie's clean-shaven face. I assumed he didn't want to have to answer questions about being alone in the woods all these months and he took my advice about shaving. I figured he wanted to be as discreet as possible. The haircut helped, too. I glanced around to keep from staring at him.

Other people were there. I saw Astrid, Danny, and their kids Beau, AJ, and Rose. There were also a few people I didn't recognize, and I figured I would end up meeting them later.

I felt underdressed. I had changed after work, and I put on shorts and a t-shirt, but I regretted it since everyone there was so beautiful and handsome at this house. There was nothing like a house full of gorgeous people to make a girl question her clothing choices. I stood up straight, trying to make the most of my casual outfit.

"I like your braids," AJ said.

"She never wears her hair like that," Charlie said.

"I like to wear braids, it's just been a while. I stopped at The Black Skillet to pick up these burgers, and my friend's mom did it for me while I was waiting."

"Hey, Hope," Astrid said from across the room. Several other people called out to me, and I waved and yelled a general greeting into the room.

"You're hanging out with us, right?" AJ turned and asked the question from over his shoulder as he walked into the kitchen.

"Yeah," I answered.

Charlie and I walked behind AJ and he reached out to give me a sideways hug. He took me into one arm, squeezing around my shoulder. I didn't know how he was planning on hugging me, and I turned and patted him on the back.

"Hey, Charlie," I said. "How are you?"

"Good. How are you? How was your day at work?"

"Fine," I said, easily. I looked straight into his dark eyes. "How are you doing with everybody being here?" I asked quietly where no one else could hear me.

"I'm fine," Charlie said. He gave me a soft smile. "Thanks for asking."

"Of course," I said, smiling. "I'm glad *you're* doing good, because I'm nervous."

"About seeing AJ?"

"About everyone being here. I'm used to it being so quiet."

"That's no reason to be nervous," he said. He reached over and touched my back. It was a reassuring, comforting gesture and his hand was only on me for a second, so I went on as if it hadn't happened.

It was Stacy who had put those thoughts in my head, and now I noticed every little thing Charlie

Morgan did and said. I felt short of breath. I hadn't even mentioned his haircut when we had a few seconds alone, and now it was too late. Everyone was around us now. I walked into the kitchen and began talking to Rose and Max as AJ set down the bag so that everyone could start digging in.

There were some extra people, and I figured out during the first couple of minutes that they were Astrid and Danny's friends. It was a couple along with their two college-age daughters.

Astrid introduced the woman as her colleague at the arts academy. Astrid was a well-known dancer who now taught and mentored high-level performers. Astrid Cameron was articulate, and I always got nervous in her presence. It helped a lot that her middle child, AJ, was a big goofball and that he liked me. He pulled me into conversations with her. AJ said what was on his mind, and he messed around with his mom even though I was intimidated by her.

AJ had a big personality, and he assumed I was there to hang out with him, so he pulled me along for the next hour or so, talking to me as we ate. It had been a while since he saw his family, so they did a lot of talking and catching up in front of me. I liked them. I loved the whole scene.

Max was there, along with two of his sons, Charlie and Casey. The girls from Chicago were there, too, and they got along with everyone. There was never a dip in the conversation—someone was always talking.

"Come with me to the pool," AJ said to me a little while later.

I smiled and touched my stomach. "Has it been thirty minutes since we ate?"

He squinted at me. "You don't care about no thirty minutes," he said playfully.

I widened my eyes at him. I could see in his eyes that he was determined, and I shrugged. "I'll go sit out there and *think* about swimming."

AJ reached out and took my hand, pulling me to my feet so we could go outside. "We're going outside if anyone wants to come with us," he announced to no one in particular.

We were the first ones on the patio, but others came out right behind us.

"Do you want to swim?" he asked, pulling me toward the pool.

"Maybe in a minute," I answered, smiling at him as I let him go.

"Come on," he said, reaching out and pulling on me again. He was smiling and he was so handsome and irresistible that I couldn't help but smile back.

"I will in a minute," I said.

"What's the difference between a minute and now?" he asked, flirting with me, tugging some more. Others came out of the house, talking and minding their own business. I glanced behind us and saw that Charlie wasn't minding his business. He was looking at me. He had walked out with his cousin, Beau, but Beau walked off, and Charlie was now standing by himself, looking at me.

I turned back to AJ who was still waiting for my answer about getting in the pool. "Hang on," I said to him. "Hang on just one second. I'll be right back."

Chapter 10

"Are you and AJ getting in the pool?" Rose asked as I crossed the patio.

"He is," I said, smiling at her as I made my way toward Charlie. "I probably will, too, in a little while."

I faced Charlie again and smiled at him as I approached. I spoke in a quiet, discreet tone as I came up to him. "I didn't know if you wanted to talk about having been out here lately. That's why I wasn't coming up to you, trying to act like we were BFFs or anything. I thought people would know we've been hanging out all this time if we're too buddy-buddy in front of them."

"Yeah, I get it," he said. "And you came here expecting to hang out with AJ."

"I'm hanging out with everybody," I said.

"He's coming up behind you," Charlie said stiffly and quietly. "He's telling me to be quiet so you won't know he's coming."

I barely had time to take in what he was saying and brace myself before I felt AJ grab me from behind. I gave a little squeal from sheer surprise, all the while trying not to cause a scene. Before I knew what was happening, AJ was holding me in his arms, walking me toward the pool. I was still because I knew squirming would make it worse.

"AJ please," I begged, latching onto him and trying to remain calm. He did not have a shirt on, and I put the pieces together about my near future. "Are you planning on jumping into the pool with me?" I asked, trying to remain calm.

AJ didn't answer me. Instead, he made a crazed face and walked toward the pool, picking up the pace as we went that way. I heard other people yelling out at us—yelling playfully at AJ to put me down. But I knew I was going in. At that point, the best I could do was hang onto AJ for dear life and try to make the next few seconds as easy and graceful for myself as possible.

Beau took his brother's lead and pulled one of the Chicago girls into the pool with him. Our fates were sealed, and soon, we were soaked. She and I found each other in the pool right after that and were able to commiserate with one another about everything that had just happened. I didn't have the chance to speak with her while we were eating, and she was a nice girl. Sophie was her name.

Others got in the pool after we did, and we spent the next hour or two playing, talking, and hanging out. It was a gorgeous afternoon, and after we swam, we went out to the lake and watched the sunset.

Charlie was around us all evening, and there were several times when I had to catch myself from saying something too familiar with him. As far as I had heard, the family hadn't brought up Savannah or the fact that Charlie was still mourning her loss. I wanted to be considerate of him, and I thought that a connection between us would only indicate how devastated he had been. I felt for Charlie, though, and I checked on him several times during the evening. He swam some, and he was always talking to someone which made me feel happy.

It was 9pm, and there were only five or six of us still hanging out when I called it a night. "I have to go," I said to AJ.

"Aw, really?"

"I have to work tomorrow."

"It's Saturday," he said.

"I know, but I have to go in for a morning shift."

"I'll walk you to your car," he said.

I nodded. "Bye everybody," I called.

And just like that, AJ and I started walking toward my car. I waved at a few people and hugged Max who was standing by the door on my way out.

"Bye Charlie!" I called since he wasn't looking at me.

He glanced at me and waved. I waved back and walked away, but I couldn't shake the feeling that Charlie wanted to say something to me. There was something different in his stare. I thought he must've been sad with me for being distant all night, but I told him it was for his own good that I was doing it, and he seemed to agree with that.

"Are you all right?" AJ asked.

"Yeah, why, what do you mean?"

"You're just being quiet. You seem like you're thinking a bunch."

"No, no I'm good. Like I was saying, work has been busy this week, so I've been tired. But it's all good."

AJ reached for my hand as we came close to my car. It was a tell-tale sign of what was to come. He would hold my hand for the next two steps and then pull me into his arms, and… yep.

"AJ, I had fun tonight," I said. I took control of our movements, leaning forward to place a quick unexpected kiss on his cheek before pulling away. "Thanks for walking me out."

"Hey, no problem. I wanted to. Thanks for coming over." He grinned at me and moved in a little, and I wanted to melt. He was a master, and I felt weak in the knees. But I kept seeing Charlie's face in my mind. I kept thinking back to how he looked at me. I kept wondering if it made him sad that I was out there with AJ.

"I'm going to head out," I said, pulling away again with a small, somewhat regretful smile.

"Okay, are you sure?" he asked.

He was handsome, and he was used to women melting as a result of his stare. But I couldn't let myself melt. And I didn't want a lot of time to pass before AJ went back out there with everyone else. I didn't want Charlie to see that he was gone for too long.

"Thanks for having me."

"Thanks for saving the day with those burgers," he said. "Uncle Max was a little mad about that meat."

I shook my head and smiled dazedly at the thought of all the wasted meat. They had planned on barbequing, but the ribs smelled funny, and no one wanted to chance it. AJ had mentioned me coming over, and that was what led to me bringing burgers for everyone.

"Okay, well, goodnight, AJ. Thanks again for having me over."

"Do you want to come back again tomorrow?"

I widened my eyes and shrugged. "Maybe," I said.

"Maybe for lunch?" he asked.

"I don't get off until noon, but I can just text you if… I'll just text you tomorrow morning, and we'll try to work something out."

"Sounds good," he said.

AJ didn't try to kiss me again. He was too smooth for that. He got the picture that I wasn't going to let it happen like it happened last time, and he left me in the driveway like he didn't care to try. He patted the top of my car and we waved at each other, and just like that, I was heading out of Broken Arrow.

I drove for twenty minutes without looking at my phone, but I took it out when I came to a blinking traffic light. I had two texts and a missed call from Stacy, and I shook my head as I called her back.

"How'd it go?" was how she answered the phone.

"Fine. Good. They liked the burgers. Everybody said how good they were."

"Are you getting married to AJ Cameron?"

"No."

"Did you hang out with him?" she asked.

"Yes. We hung out. He jumped into the pool with me."

Stacy squealed, and I laughed, flinched, and held the phone away from my ear.

"With your clothes on?"

"Yes, my clothes were on. Thank goodness I didn't have my phone in my pocket."

"That's amazing. I saw a picture of him from the other day and he is sooo hot, Hope."

"Charlie got his haircut."

"Yeah, Charlie was there. How did that go with you hanging out with AJ?"

"It was fine. Me and Charlie are just friends. I barely talked to him at all. I didn't think everyone knew how long he had been here, so I pretended we weren't so well acquainted."

"So well acquainted?" she asked. "What the heck do you mean by that?"

"I didn't know if everyone knew he'd been staying out there so long. His dad and his brother obviously know, but even they didn't say anything to him about it, at least not in front of me. They just act like they're all meeting there and don't even talk about Savannah."

"And Charlie was just fine with you ignoring him and hanging out with AJ?"

"Of course he was fine. Why wouldn't he be?"

"What happened besides y'all jumping into the pool? Did you hold hands? Did you kiss?"

"Stacy, you are shameless."

"Because I get no action over here. I'm stuck in this restaurant, and all the hot guys want to hook up with you or Tabitha." (Tabitha was a woman who worked at the restaurant.)

"Neither happened," I said. "We didn't hold hands or kiss. He reached out for my hand a couple of times but it was just to get me to go somewhere."

"Did he try to kiss you? At the end of the night."

"Kind of. I think he would've. He walked me to my car."

"But you didn't do it?"

"No. Why?"

"That's what *you* should be answering. Why didn't you kiss him?"

"Why do you care? I just didn't feel like doing it. I don't know why."

"I will never know what in the world came over you in this moment, Hope Jones. I will never understand you. AJ Cameron? You dissed him? He'll probably never wanna hang out with you again."

"He does. He said he did. I'm supposed to maybe go over there tomorrow."

"When? After work?"

"Yes, tomorrow afternoon."

"Goodness gracious, Hope. Do better tomorrow than you did tonight. Please don't screw it up."

"Okay fine," I said, even though I planned on making my own decisions.

"Let me know how it goes, please. And if you ever want me to go over there with you I would love to."

But as she spoke, my phone began ringing on the other line. I could hear the tone cutting in over what she was saying.

"Hey, my phone's ringing. It's probably my mom," I said.

"Okay, I'll talk to you later."

I was driving and I tried to hang up and pick up the other line without taking my eyes off of the road.

"Hello?" I said, hoping I had pushed the button. I was on a backroad and I looked away for a second, just long enough to glance at the screen.

Charlie.

It wasn't my mom at all.

I pressed the green button. "Hello?"

Chapter 11

"Hey, hello, are you there?" I asked, hoping I had succeeded in answering the call. "Charlie?"

"Yeah, I'm here," Charlie said.

I smiled at the sound of his familiar voice over my speaker.

"What are you doing?" I asked.

"A few people are still down at the pool, but I came inside. What are you doing?"

"I'm still driving. I'm about ten minutes from my apartment."

"AJ said you were coming back tomorrow."

"He mentioned that before I left. I have to work until noon, but maybe after that."

There was a pause. I waited for him to respond but he hesitated.

"I'm thinking about driving over there," he said, finally. "Would you want to hang out for a little while if I do?"

"You're coming to Graham Springs?"

"Yes."

"Oh, well, of course I would want to hang out. When are you coming?"

"Oh, I was talking about right now."

"Really? Oh, yeah, that's fine."

I glanced at the clock. It was after nine, and I had to be at work at eight in the morning, but I didn't care.

"Come on. Do you want to meet me at The Black Skillet?"

"Are they open?" he asked.

"They are. They're open late on weekends. But I'd be fine going to a park or the lake or something."

"Yeah, we could take a walk."

"Okay, that's a better idea," I said.

"You can actually just come to my apartment in that case. We have a trail that leads down to the lake. It's a half-mile, and it's nice."

"Okay. I've never been to your apartment at night, and never when you weren't with me, so you might need to text me your address."

"No problem. I'll text it to you right now. Uh, Charlie, is, is everything okay? Were you just coming to… hang out?"

My tone was wary, and he assured me. "Yeah, oh, yeah, I'm… nothing's wrong. I just wanted to go for a drive, and I thought you might want to hang out together if I drove over there."

"I do. Yeah. I do want to."

"Okay, great. I'm going to leave here in like five minutes, so I'll see you soon."

"I'm texting my address."

We hung up, and Charlie was at my apartment in no time. I got home and took a quick shower to rinse the pool water off of me, and then I cleaned my apartment—and before I knew it, I heard a knock on my door.

"Come in!" I called.

"What's up," Charlie said, coming in.

"What's up with you?" I replied from the kitchen. My laundry closet was in my kitchen and I closed the folding door just as he came inside. "I was picking up some clothes," I continued. "I took a shower when I got home."

He crossed to my kitchen, and I smiled at him. He made my apartment look small. He had filled out some in the last few months. He had on a shirt that seemed a little tighter on him than it was last month. It was a cream-colored shirt with a faded fishing logo on the front. I read the logo, staring at the shapes of his chest underneath. I had seen him without the shirt earlier in the night, and I had been a little distracted by his chest then and now.

I tore my eyes off of him. Stacy had me all wound up about kissing men—I told myself that was the only reason I was noticing Charlie's chest, and his arms, and his mouth. I continued looking away, busying myself in the kitchen.

"Would you like something to drink?" I asked.

"Water is good," he said.

I grabbed two glasses out of the cupboard and filled one of them with filtered water from the fridge before handing it to him.

"Thank you," he said.

He took it from me and during the transfer, our hands barely brushed.

What was wrong with me? We touched each other all the time. We were friends and we hung out all the time. *And now I'm noticing when his hand touches two of my fingers?* I thought of Stacy and the fact that I wouldn't be aware of any of this had she not been hyping me up.

Then I remembered Savannah, and I remembered I couldn't be with Charlie. I thought of her, and again I saw Charlie as only a friend.

"You did really good tonight," I said, feeling proud of him. "And your hair looks great. I didn't get to say anything, but I really like it."

Charlie ran his hand through his hair. It was shorter now, but not as short as it used to be.

"It's a nice haircut," I said. "It makes you look fancy, like you should've come over here on a yacht."

Charlie smiled. "I have yacht hair? I'm not sure if that's a compliment."

"Sure it is. Yacht-anything is a compliment."

"Your face, too," I said.

Charlie rubbed his jaw. "I have a yacht face?" he asked reluctantly.

I laughed. "No, you shaved. I was noticing you shaved, but I didn't get to mention it. It looks good. You've been working your way there, anyway, getting shorter last week."

He nodded since my assessment was accurate.

"Do you want to go walking?" I asked.

"Sure," he said. He tilted his head back and drained his glass before setting it on the counter next to him.

"Right now?" I asked.

He shrugged. "I'm not in a big hurry. What's this? I noticed it the other day when I was here, but I didn't ask." Charlie pointed at a small painting of a flower on my kitchen wall.

"It's by one of our little patients," I said. "She's got a bunch of health stuff going on, so we see her regularly. Oh, I've told you about her. Little Jade. She painted that for me for Christmas last year."

"And this?" he asked, pointing at a cartoon drawing on my fridge that was drawn with a ballpoint pen on a napkin from Stacy's restaurant. It was a character—a hot-pepper-looking character, but he had a face and arms and legs. He was riding a skateboard.

"That's by Landon."

"Did he copy it off of something?" he asked.

"No, he likes to draw food with faces. I think on the other side there's a…" I reached up and took the napkin off of the fridge and turned it over. There was a drawing of a long, skinny churro with a top hat. I flashed it at Charlie and he laughed.

"He was trying to get me to eat Mexican food, can you tell?"

"It's on a napkin from the burger place, so I guess it didn't work," he said.

"No, he drew those over here. He actually got the napkin out of that drawer." I pointed to the napkin drawer which was close to the refrigerator.

"Did you end up going for Mexican that night?" he asked.

"How could I refuse?" I said.

"That's funny. Those are both cool drawings."

"Those girls were nice today. Sophie and Kara. They were, I don't mean this to sound weird, but they were nicer than I thought they would be from their looks."

"You thought they looked basic?"

"Not basic. They were just so pretty that I thought they might be… b-basic, I guess," I said, smiling and shaking my head at him.

"You're prettier than them," he said.

But I was already saying something else and we talked over each other. "But they weren't basic at all. I liked them. They were nice. I'm always so nervous around your aunt, though. She wears those robes that make her look like she's in some kind of movie—the Great Gatsby or something. She needs a long cigarette."

Charlie laughed. "I know, I don't know why that lake house equals silk robes for Aunt Astrid. I've seen her in Florida, Houston, and Chicago—other places too. But she really only wears those robes when we're over here. I don't think I've seen her in them otherwise."

"Still, I bet her regular clothes are equally intimidating," I said, laughing.

"You don't act intimidated," he said, cutting his eyes at me.

I shrugged. "I'm faking it in front of them."

"What about in front of me?" he asked. He glanced at me and I crossed my eyes and stuck my tongue out in a non-flattering pose, and he laughed at me.

"You're my Charlie," I said. "I could never be scared of you." Even in this moment, I was highly intimidated. But I faked it, smiling at him after I made a face. "Do you want to go for a walk?" I asked.

He nodded at me, and we started moving. We walked slowly, and my apartment was a good distance from the lake, so it took us fifteen minutes to make our way to the shore. We talked continually. There was never a break in the conversation which flowed easily and naturally. We talked about video games and movies. Charlie was my age, and we were exposed to a lot of the same games and pop culture growing up. We debated which Mario Kart was the best.

"I have no idea where I am," he said, finally, looking out at the lake.

I wasn't sure of the context.

"What do you mean?" I asked.

"On the lake. If I got in a boat, I don't think I could get back to the property from here."

"Sure you can. Just stay left. Except for that one little loop by the canal, but otherwise, stay left. You would start to recognize the property as you got over in that direction."

He laughed. "I would not," he said. "Not at night. And I would take that wrong left that you warned me about. I have no idea where the canal is."

"I think you could do it. If your life depended on it and it was just you in a boat, I think you could do it."

"Oh definitely, under those circumstances. If my life depended on it. I could swim if I had to."

"What about for a thousand dollars?" I asked.

"Swim to Broken Arrow? No."

"How about if you go by boat?"

He made a face like he was considering it. "At night?"

"Of course, at night."

"I might do it for a thousand," he agreed thoughtfully. "Why? Are you trying to whip up a grand to get me to try my boating skills?"

"Would you really take a thousand from me?"

"Would you really go so far as to have me boat across the Pacific Ocean just to test my skills?"

"You live on the real ocean," I said. "Don't even try to make me think you're scared of little old Lake Sutton."

"I'm not scared of this lake. I'll take you over there and back tonight if you've got a boat."

"I don't have a boat. Dad sold his, and my mom doesn't live anywhere near the lake. If I did, I would be tempted, though. I might test your skills."

"I would definitely not hesitate to do it with you in the boat. If I got lost, you would just tell me where to go."

The trail had led us to a small public park with lakefront access. There was a playground with a set of swings, a slide, and one of those metal merry-go-rounds that were notorious for making kids dizzy and nauseated.

"I love those things," I said, pointing to it. "I used to get my brother to push me as fast as he could, and I would never get dizzy," I said.

"What about now?" Charlie asked. I shook my head at him. "No, actually. Landon pushed me on it the other day, and I was fine. I don't mind it. He said it was because I lay with my head near the middle, but either way, I don't get dizzy"

"You rode this the other day?" Charlie asked, climbing onto it and laying down. He looked at me with a smile, and I shrugged a shoulder.

"Not the other day, but recently. A few weeks ago, maybe."

Charlie smiled at me as he slowly pushed himself with his foot. "I'm pretty sure I could take Landon pushing me on this thing without losing my lunch," he said.

"Oh, you think so?" I asked. "What about Hope? I'm faster than Landon."

Charlie picked his head up and looked at me with a skeptical expression.

"Watch your feet," I said. I ran with him for five or six paces and then I stopped, tossing the metal pole out of my hand in a practiced pushing movement to maximize the speed of the merry-go-round.

Push,

push,

push.

I sent it flying with hard, practiced pushes to the metal poles as they flew by me. I spun them vigorously, giving Charlie several fast rotations before pulling back and taking my hands away. I watched Charlie's calm face as he spun. He was focused on the trees above him. I reached out to gently slow the big metal wheel until it came to a stop.

I strategically stopped Charlie when he came back around to where his feet were close to me. He sat up with a smile, but his face suddenly grew serious, and he braced himself and swayed like he might get sick. His joke only lasted for a second, and I was barely reaching out to help him before he smiled again. I pulled back and slapped him gently on the shoulder.

"I thought you were really sick," I said.

"I'm fine," he said, grinning. "I don't love getting dizzy, but it doesn't make me feel sick or anything."

"What about slides?" I asked.

"What about them?"

"How do you feel about them?" He gave a slight shrug. "About the same as I do about the spinning thing," he said nonchalantly.

"Swings?"

He shrugged again. "Slightly better," he said uncertainly.

"Swings it is, then," I said.

Chapter 12

Charlie and I stayed on the playground for an hour before heading back up the path toward my apartment again. A couple of people had come and gone while we were down at the lakeside park, but we never talked to anyone else.

"What time is it?" I asked as we came to my apartment complex.

"It's after eleven," he said without looking at his watch to make sure. "I know you need to be up early. I didn't mean to keep you."

"No, it was fun," I said.

I looked at him as we meandered slowly down the path. It was quiet out, aside from the sound of frogs or cicadas or whatever it was chirping in the woods.

"I'm glad you came over," I added. "Next time you'll have to take me back to Broken Arrow in a boat."

"At night?"

"Yeah," I said.

"For a thousand?"

"Yeah, sure," I said, nodding and shrugging like it was a possibility for me to pay someone a grand for such a thing, which it wasn't.

"Okay, I'll do it for a thousand," he said with a deadpan expression.

"I'll have to put it on layaway," I said. "I'll get on a payment plan."

"I'll just do it one night, and then you can owe me a thousand in goods and services over like the next few months or so."

I laughed, knowing we were joking. "Thank goodness you're going back to Miami."

"Thanks a lot," he said sarcastically.

"No, I just meant I'll get out of my responsibilities—the theoretical thousand dollars. I won't be happy to see you go, Charlie."

"Are you thinking about coming out to the house tomorrow?"

"Yeah, maybe. We talked about it. I mean, I guess I'll text AJ in the morning and see what he has going on…" I trailed off and shrugged awkwardly. I didn't know what to say, honestly. I felt uneasy about the whole AJ thing now.

"You don't have to wait on AJ to invite you," Charlie said. "You can come over because I invited you. I'm better friends with you than AJ is, anyway."

"I know, but your family already saw me there with him. And I already told him I was going to go tomorrow, so I'll probably head over there after I get off of work."

I stooped down and picked up a rock.

I started to sense a little tension radiating off of Charlie at the mention of AJ, and it made me feel some type of way. I felt like he was jealous, and the idea of it caused a warm gushing sensation to happen in my core. I had wanted Charlie so badly that my body automatically responded even though having him was no longer an option. He was such a good man, but my ability to have feelings for him turned off when I found out he was married. I could appreciate him for the wonderful, funny, dependable, sweet, handsome, masculine, amazing man he was and still be aware of the fact that I would not end up with him in the long run.

But I wasn't going to end up with AJ in the long run either. And if I was going to end up with neither of them, it didn't matter who I kissed. I told myself that kissing Charlie was the same as kissing AJ—no harm, no foul.

I thought of kissing Charlie, and my stomach started to feel funny again. I looked at his face and I suddenly felt like I really wanted to do it. My heart raced, and I was glad he couldn't hear my thoughts. We headed toward the parking lot, and I knew we would find our way to his truck. There was a picnic area to our left, and Charlie's truck was straight ahead and toward the right.

Charlie hesitated when we came to the path that led to the picnic area. There was a large gazebo off to the side. I wasn't sure if gazebos came in different shapes, but this was one of the round ones. It was a nice one, actually. It was painted white and there was some kind of flowering vine growing all over it. The apartment complex was called "The Gazebo" and this very structure was their mascot and logo.

The owners really kept it looking nice. It was large enough for ten or twelve people to sit comfortably, but it was empty now.

I followed Charlie as he walked toward it.

"What's going on with you and AJ?" he asked as we took the path. He kept walking, going inside the gazebo and looking around. I was taken aback by his question and I took a second to think of how I wanted to answer it.

"Nothing actually. What you saw was all that happened. We're just friends. I rarely come in here," I added as we made our way inside. "When I first moved into this place, I thought I would be coming in here having a picnic every day, and I think I've come in here like three or four times in two years."

"Hope."

"Yes?"

"AJ dates other girls when he goes to Chicago."

I grinned and pulled back, looking at Charlie with a sly expression. "What would he say if he knew his cousin was ratting him out?" I said, messing around with Charlie.

"It's no secret," he said. "He kissed you tonight, and I just didn't want you to think you're the only one."

"Gee, thanks, Charlie. One, I knew that already. And two, I didn't even kiss him. If I would've kissed him, though, it would've been with full knowledge that I am not the only person he has ever done that with. AJ is all over social media."

"Well, just so you're aware of what you're getting into. And he came back grinning from ear to ear after he walked you out tonight, so don't try to act like nothing happened."

I pulled back staring at Charlie unable to decide if I had heard him correctly. I stood right in front of him. He was taller than me, but I stared up at him, not backing down.

"Are you saying you think I'm lying?" I asked. "Do you think I'm lying about kissing AJ?"

"Did you do it or not?"

"No, I didn't."

"I thought you did because he walked you outside, and then he came back grinning and talking about how you were coming back tomorrow."

"Did you call me and come over here to ask me that?" I asked, still staring up at him.

"No, I came over here to hang out, and I just happen to be asking you that."

"Well AJ walked me out, and nothing happened, Charlie. We said goodbye."

I did not expect it. Maybe I should've expected it given our proximity, but it was a complete surprise when Charlie ducked and softly let his lips hit mine. He let his mouth stay there for two soft, glorious heartbeats. My heart. *Was it even beating?* Then he pulled back, staring at me again. Charlie Morgan's mouth had been on mine and I… Could. Not. Breathe.

I held my breath as long as I could, and then I let it out, looking away, breaking our gaze. I was looking away, but I felt him start to duck, and saw his face start to come toward mine, and there was nothing I could do to stop myself from going to him again. We kissed again. It was mutual. It was oh so mutual. Charlie had shaved and his mouth was… goodness, I could feel some stubble even though his beard was shaved, and my mouth was on fire. My body was on fire. This kiss was different. This was… I couldn't think straight. I couldn't breathe. I could do nothing but feel.

Charlie kissed me three or four times—all of them slow, lingering, perfect kisses. And then he gently opened his mouth, sucking, tugging my lip. I only felt it happen for a second, but it was a gut-wrenching second. My lip was in Charlie's warm mouth, and it was too much to handle. I felt like I might shatter into a million bits.

He pulled back. Out of my periphery, I could see his chest as it rose and fell. Charlie. He was clean-shaven and he looked just like the old boy I knew. He was so handsome that I could hardly bear to look at his face. His lips had been on mine, and my body was wild feeling as a result of it. I was having all sorts of physical sensations I had never felt before.

I smiled and wiped my lips. People could see into the gazebo, but not well, and I didn't care anyway. Charlie Morgan had kissed me, and I did not regret it at all. I hoped he didn't regret it.

I tried to read his facial expression.

"I didn't want you to be kissed by no one tonight," he said. I gave him a curious look, and he continued, "I definitely didn't want you to be kissed by two guys. But I also didn't want you to be kissed by no one."

"You were hoping I would kiss someone tonight?" I asked, smiling at him.

"Yes, but only one person. One specific person."

"I did only kiss one person tonight," I said, nodding dazedly and wiping my mouth again with the back of my hand. "I'm not sure if it was the right, specific person you had in mind, but…"

"Yes, it was," he agreed.

"W-well, I was pretty fine with it."

"I was, too," Charlie said. "I'm letting you go inside so you can get some rest, okay?"

"Okay," I said, trying not to glance at his perfect mouth.

"I don't know what to say about AJ. He's only going to be at the house for a week, so I don't know what to tell you. It's your choice, ultimately, if or when or how you hang out with him."

"Do you not want me to hang out with AJ?" I asked.

"It's your decision what you do."

"Nothing happened between us tonight, and he was cool about it."

"It's whatever you want to do, really. I don't mean to put you on the spot. He's a good guy, and you can hang out with him if you want. I wasn't trying to rat him out earlier."

"Well, are you trying to get me to hang out with him now? Do you regret what we just..." I trailed off, and Charlie spoke.

"No, no, good grief, no. I'm just saying, I get it if you still want to hang out with AJ."

"I'll just tell him I can't make it tomorrow, and then hang back for a week or so," I said. "I don't want anything to be awkward with any of us."

"I'm not awkward," Charlie said easily.

"I know you're not," I replied. "You're anything but awkward." He was Charlie. He was natural and easy, and he snuck in another kiss before turning to walk out of the gazebo. He kissed me on the mouth, and then he walked away, leaving me breathless.

We were in the darkness outside, but Charlie was framed by white wood and greenery. I took a moment to appreciate the magic of it all before forcing myself back to reality. *What had happened? What had we just done?*

It was a world-shattering kiss.

My world was shattered.

I liked Charlie a lot, but this thing between us just wouldn't work.

I wasn't ready for any of this.

I was glad AJ was in town and I had a week to think about it.

Chapter 13

Three days later

"Your dinner is on the house tonight, Hope," Bridgette said as I came into The Black Skillet that afternoon after work.

"For what?" I asked.

"Candice was beside herself with baby Aaron last night. He was miserable with those little ears."

"I know," I said. "Doctor Warner said his ears were pretty bad."

"Candice said they were some of the worst the doctor had ever seen. He gave him a shot and some medicine to take at home. I think Candice already went and picked it up from the pharmacy. She said Aaron's feeling a lot better already from that shot. She was so thankful y'all got him in early this morning. That's why your dinner is on the house tonight."

"Oh, Dr. Warner was happy to fit him in, Ms. Bridgette."

"Yeah, but he wouldn't have gotten them in so early if it wasn't for you working there. I really appreciate how sweet and kind y'all are to little Aaron. Candice loves your office. You go ahead and order whatever you want tonight, and I'm not going to put it on your tab."

"Thank you, Ms. Bridgette. I'll just take a burger if you don't mind."

"Stacy's in the back," she said when she saw me look around.

"Some of those Morgan boys are back there, eating in the bar area."

"Which ones?" I asked, doing my best to seem casual.

She shrugged and made a guilty face. "I can't tell them apart," she said. "There's a few back there, though. Max is here, the man from Florida, and a couple of the ones who are your age."

"Two guys?" I asked, craning my neck and trying to look back there.

She nodded. "Three including Max."

I took a measured breath, trying to calm the nerves that hit me instantly. I had been thinking about Charlie Morgan for three days. My thoughts were sporadic and changing, but I thought of him a lot. I had not heard from him at all. I had told AJ I couldn't make it over there to visit with him, and that was the last I heard from either of them.

"You should go back there," Bridgette said.

I wasn't sure what I should do, but her offer made me start heading that way. I saw Stacy when I rounded the corner and she made eye contact with me before smiling and waving me over.

She was at a booth with Max, Casey, and AJ. There was no Charlie, and I felt instantly deflated.

"Hey guys," I said, smiling as I headed their way. It was early for dinner, and the restaurant wasn't busy, but I could tell by the empty plates that they were wrapping up.

"Did you come for dinner?" Max asked.

"I'm just picking it up to take home," I said.

"Come sit for a minute until we get up," he said, motioning to the seat next to him.

I moved around Stacy, hugging her briefly in the process. Casey and AJ were sitting opposite me, and I smiled at them as I got settled into the booth.

"Charlie would have been here with us, but he's injured," Max said.

"He would have been miserable with how choppy that water was on the way here," Casey added before I could say anything.

"What happened to him?" I asked, feeling like I couldn't breathe until I knew more.

"Old football injury," AJ said.

"New football injury," Max corrected smiling. "His quad—his leg. They were playing catch with a football in the yard, and he slipped and pulled it."

"To be fair, it was raining, and we were all over the place in that game," Casey said. "I'm surprised he was the only one injured."

"Is he okay?" I asked, looking seriously at Max. "I haven't talked to him in a few days. I figured he was busy, but I didn't know he was hurt."

Max shook his head. "This happened last night," he said.

I wasn't sure why I mentioned that I hadn't talked to him in a few days. I felt odd for saying it in front of them, and I stared into space as I said something to change the subject. "I hope his leg is okay. You should take him a burger."

"We are," Max said. He looked at me. "I like your pirate ship shirt."

I looked down at my scrubs. "It's one of my most complimented tops," I said. I laughed. "I seriously do get high praises from our little patients."

"We should have gone to your clinic for Charlie's leg," Max said.

I looked at him with a curious expression. "Was it bad enough that he had to see a doctor?"

"No, no, I'm just joking, he's okay. He's just hobbling around on it. He'll rest it and be fine."

It seemed as though Max was bringing up Charlie on purpose. He had done it twice, and both times, he looked at me and seemed interested in my reaction. I wondered if he knew what happened between us. I wondered if I looked guilty. I asked them what boat they came on, and that got us talking about different boats for a little while.

AJ said he and some others would be taking the bigger boat out with some big pull-behind toys the following day. He asked if I wanted to go. I thanked him and told him I wish I could but explained that I had to work all day, which was the truth. AJ acted a little disappointed, and I tried not to notice without seeming insensitive.

Stacy had left and she came back with their ticket and boxes along with my food, and within minutes, we were all heading toward the door. I stayed back and talked to Stacy, but several people had come into the restaurant so I wasn't there for very long.

I went straight to my house to change and eat and then from there to Landon's. He was leaving tomorrow to go to Nashville to see my brother, and I had some things to send with him.

"A whole box?" Landon asked, reaching out for the load I was carrying when he opened the door.

"Eric didn't tell you? He asked me to pack all this stuff from Mom's house."

"He told me you were bringing over a few things."

"I barely got it into that box," I said.

"I feel that," Landon said referring to how heavy it was.

"Yeah, it's packed. There's clothes and a Wii. There's even a lava lamp."

"Sounds like a dangerous combination," he said, setting it down carefully.

"I packed it really well," I said. "I don't think anything's going to break unless you go tossing it around."

"Why don't you come with me?" he asked.

"I thought about it, but I'd have to take off work."

"So, what? You never take off. Call in sick. It's only four more days and then we're on the weekend. I can have you back by next Monday."

"Four days is a lot for Doctor Warner. Plus, Eric doesn't have room for both of us."

"You can have the couch and I'll take the floor," Landon offered.

"Just go," I said. "I kind of regret not going, but it's too late for me to decide that now."

"No, it's really not!" he begged. "Come onnnn…"

"No, I can't, I didn't mean to make you think I could," I said. "I wouldn't do that to Dr. Warner. We've already got a nurse on vacation."

I also had Charlie on my mind. I was blaming work, but I needed to check on Charlie. They had said his injury wasn't a big deal, but I had honestly expected to hear something from him after what happened between us in the gazebo, and I found myself wondering why he didn't call.

I was comfortable at Landon's place, and I took my telephone out of my back pocket so that I could sit on his couch.

I went to toss it onto the coffee table and I saw Charlie's name on my screen. He had called. The little phone symbol was next to his name, and I knew I had missed a call.

"Hey, I didn't realize I missed a call," I said to Landon.

"I need to go get some laundry out of the dryer, anyway," Landon said, nodding. "I can't find my socks, and I need them for climbing."

"I'll make this call while you go do that, and then we'll climb."

Landon took off, and I pressed the button to call Charlie. My heart rate sped up as I waited for him to pick up the phone.

"Hello?" I said when I heard him answer. "I had a missed call but there was no message. Was it a butt dial?"

"What, no, it was a finger dial."

"What are you doing?" I asked. "I heard you hurt your leg."

"Yeah, Dad told me he saw you. My leg's not that big of a deal, I just didn't want to go out on those waves. I would have come if I would have known you were at the restaurant."

"I was looking for you when I saw your dad," I said, feeling jittery. "I was sad you weren't there."

"I miss talking to you," he said.

"I was thinking that same thing. I was wondering why I hadn't heard from you."

"I thought you would call me," he said.

"I thought you would call me," I returned.

"Where are you?" he asked.

"Landon's. We're about to climb on his wall for a little while. He's leaving for Nashville in the morning. He's going to see my brother. I brought some stuff over here."

Landon must have gone to the laundry room as fast as he could because he was already back.

"Yeah, I'm going to Nashville and I'm trying to get Hope to come with me," Landon said, speaking loudly so Charlie could hear him. "Who is it?" Landon asked, not knowing.

"Charlie," I said.

"What'd he say?" Charlie asked.

"He said he was trying to get me to go with him to Nashville tomorrow, but I already told him I had to stay and work. As much as I want to see my brother, I just can't go on such short notice."

"So, you're staying in town?" Charlie asked.

"Yeah, yeah, there was never any question. I just came over here to bring my brother's stuff. I wish I could go, but I can't."

"Hey, can I see you tonight?"

My heart pounded.

"Yes," I replied instantly, not caring where, when, or how.

"I'll come over there," he said.

"Sure," I answered. "What time?"

"One hour?"

"Sure," I said. "My place. I'll still be sweaty because we'll probably climb for forty-five minutes."

"Do you want me to hold back longer?" he asked.

"No," I said.

"Okay. I'll see you soon.

"Okay."

I hung up with him. I smiled as nonchalantly as I could to Landon, but my insides were all stirred up after talking to Charlie.

"Charlie," I said to Landon. "Morgan. Charlie Morgan."

"I know what Charlie," he said. "Is he going to your house?"

"Yeah, after we climb for a little while," I said. "Are you ready? Did you find your socks?"

Chapter 14

Charlie Morgan

It was understandable that Hope would need some time to think about what had happened with her and Charlie. That was why he hadn't called. He also didn't want her to come back over to the house while AJ was visiting. He saw how his cousin looked at Hope.

Charlie had decided to give Hope time to think about everything, but he wished she would have reached out to him this week. Max ran into her at the burger place in Graham Springs today, and he told Charlie that Hope seemed like she wanted to talk to him. He had been busy with his family visiting, but he still had time to miss her. Charlie was excited when his dad came home saying that Hope seemed interested.

He hadn't planned on asking if he could go to her house. He did that by instinct when he realized she was over at Landon's house. He had feelings about it, and they weren't good feelings. He knew the two of them were just friends, but he felt weird about her being over there, and that was what made him ask if they could see each other.

Charlie arrived in Graham Springs a few minutes early, and he parked near Hope's apartment building and walked over to the white gazebo. He could clearly picture the scene they shared last time. He could imagine the feel of her skin against his.

Charlie had done a lot of soul searching in the last three months, and Hope had been a gigantic part of it. Spending time with her was how his healing had begun. He had been in a pit before that. She was innocent and kind, and she saw the good in everyone. And she was beautiful.

He thought of Savannah. If you had asked him, he would have never said that he would be ready to love again this soon after losing Savannah. But he had no other choice but to love Hope. He had fallen in love with her, and it was beyond his control. He knew if he didn't try to keep her he would regret it. So, there he was, sitting in a gazebo, waiting for her to come home. She would be coming from another guy's house, but he wasn't going to think about that.

Charlie sat there for fifteen minutes before Hope pulled into a parking spot. He watched as she got out. She was focused on his truck, but she turned to her apartment when she didn't see him inside. Charlie gave a sharp, quick whistle, and Hope turned his way, smiling when she realized where he was.

He waited inside the gazebo for her. His leg was still sore, and he didn't want to hobble to get to her. He waited, sitting in the round wooden structure.

There were others in the parking lot, but no one was nearby, and Charlie kicked his feet out in front of him and sat back like he owned the place. He watched her approach. She had her hair in a bun and she was wearing shorts and a t-shirt with tennis shoes She had a duffel bag over her shoulder, and her face and chest were still pink from exertion.

Charlie reacted to her on the inside, but he tried to play it cool, watching her with a smile.

"I'm so sorry I'm late," she said, rushing to him. She went straight over to the far side of the gazebo where Charlie was sitting. He stood up as she approached. "And I'm sorry I'm all sweaty," she continued. "How long have you been waiting here?" She set her bag down on the bench nearby and then she leaned in and hugged Charlie before she sat down.

"Not long," he said, answering her question.

"I'm a few minutes late. Landon and my brother were doing their best to convince me to go to Nashville."

"Is he just going for a few days? Do you think you would regret it if you don't go? I don't want you to go, I was just thinking you should if you think you'd regret missing it."

"I've asked myself that. He's going for six days, but part of it's a weekend, and technically it could work out for me to go, but sleeping arrangements aren't great, and we have a nurse at work who's out this week."

He looked at her. He wanted to kiss her right then. He wanted to take her—to have her agree that she was his and he was hers and they were together forever.

"I want you to be able to see your brother, but for what it's worth I'm glad you didn't go. I'm glad you're here right now."

"Even if I smell a little bit?" she said, smiling at him.

She had the hint of a dimple on her cheek, and Charlie stared at it thinking he wanted to look at her face for the rest of his life.

"You do not smell," he said.

He leaned over like he wanted to sample her scent, and she leaned toward him, not shying away. Charlie put his nose next to her neck and shoulder area. He smelled some kind of fresh scent of her deodorant or detergent, and then he smelled the slightest hint of sweat. It drove him wild.

"You don't stink," he said. He kept inhaling, running his nose up her neck, up her jaw and onto her cheek. "Nope," he said with certainty. His mouth was near her ear. "I'm still not smelling anything bad." He could see her chest begin to rise and fall at a quickened pace, and she put her hand out, letting her palm rest against his arm as she shifted to face him.

"Ms. Bridgette told me some of the Morgans were in the restaurant earlier, and I got all excited when I went back there thinking it was you, but then I didn't see you. I was missing you. How's your leg?"

"It's fine. It's really no big deal. I've had worse injuries."

She looked down at his leg. He had on shorts and she saw the elastic brace on one of his legs, sticking out of the shorts a little. "I was about to ask which leg it happened to, but I see it's wrapped up."

"Yep," he said. "I'd like to hear about how much you wished it was me at the restaurant."

Hope laughed and shook her head as she looked at him. "I did wish it was you, Charlie," she said. The certainty yet vulnerability in her tone lit some kind of fire within Charlie, and he did his best not to react outwardly.

"I would have probably gone with Landon tonight, honestly. He and my brother were giving me such a hard time that I almost got talked into going."

"But what?" he asked when she paused.

"But I was in a hurry to come over here and see you. I noticed what time it was, and I told them I couldn't even think about things like taking unexpected trips when I was already late for something else—somewhere I really wanted to go."

They sat next to each other in the gazebo, talking softly and staring at each other. She had on no makeup and her hair was pulled back. She was completely exposed to him, and he could see every nuance of her facial expressions. She wanted him, he could tell that. She was flirting with him.

"I was hoping you'd call me this week," he said.

"I was hoping you'd call me," Hope returned. "You were the one who has family visiting. I didn't want to interrupt y'all."

"Well, I'm the one who kissed you last time we were together, so I wanted to give you time to think about it."

"I was giving you time to think about it," she said. "I thought you regretted it."

"I can promise you, I did not regret it."

She stared at his face. "Charlie?"

"Yes, Hope?"

"I hope your leg feels better."

She ended the sentence uncertainly and he smiled and pulled back to stare at her.

"Is that what you were going to say?"

"I don't know what I was going to say," she said. He knew she wanted him, and he wanted her. They had become close in the last few months. She was a part of his life now, and being away from her these last few days made him realize he didn't want to move forward without her.

She looked at him like she thought they might kiss, and the last thing he wanted to do was let her down. He leaned in, closing the gap that remained between them. Charlie ached to touch her, and it took a great deal of restrain for him to do it patiently. He let his mouth touch hers. She was relieved to kiss him, and he did it two or three times with her smiling at him between each one. She was absolutely adorable.

"What are you thinking?" he asked.

"I'm not thinking anything," she said. "I'm just smiling because it's… fun to kiss you." She bit her lip and stared hopefully at him.

There was nothing Charlie could do to stop himself from doing it again. He pulled her over to him, and she leaned onto him, resting in his arms. Charlie held onto Hope, opening his mouth to her and kissing her deeply. She leaned into him, getting closer, holding onto him as they connected in a slow, rhythmic pulsing motion.

Charlie kissed Hope gently but with barely restrained passion, and she let out a little moan when he pulled back. He leaned in and kissed her again because of the moan, and they repeated the process a few more times. Hope made a sound every time he tried to stop, so he sat out there and continued for what must have been a half-hour but felt more like a half-second.

It was the most fun Charlie ever had kissing a woman. He had been in love with Savannah, but they had never shared a kiss like this. There would always be a place in his heart for the memory of Savannah, but Charlie couldn't help but feel like everything in the universe, like God himself had led him to this moment.

Hope was his happily ever after. She had to be.

They barely talked—they just sat there and looked at each other and kissed. It was better than perfect. The sun was setting, the light was disappearing, and neither of them wanted to be anywhere else but in that gazebo. Charlie and Hope connected sweetly and lovingly. She was exquisite, and Charlie could not fathom that she was the girl who had always been at the lake house in Arkansas.

He felt like he needed to have her with him all the time now. He had to let her know where he stood. Charlie thought of how he felt during the last few days compared to how he felt right now, and he knew he never wanted to be apart from Hope again.

Chapter 15

Hope Jones

Charlie Morgan had kissed me like he was my boyfriend. He had kissed me like I had never been kissed before—like I didn't even know was possible.

I stared in the mirror at my own mouth, looking to see if there was any proof that we kissed for such a long time. I had come into my bathroom to take a shower and change, and Charlie was in the living room waiting for me. I didn't know why I expected my mouth to still be pink or swollen, but I looked in the mirror, anyway.

Inspecting my own mouth made me remember his kiss, I pictured it and I felt a yearning sensation as a result. I quickly finished combing my hair and then I towel-dried it one last time before heading out to meet Charlie. He was sitting on my couch, and he started to get up.

"Stay and rest your leg and I'll come sit by you."

My apartment was small, and I made it to Charlie quickly. I looked at him after I sat next to him. "Do you need an ice pack or anything?" I asked.

"No, thank you. I'll do all that when I get back to the house. Hey, I was thinking you could come over tomorrow even though AJ is still there."

"What? No. He's only got a few more days."

"I know, but I don't want to wait a few more days to see you. And you might have fun coming out and going onto the water with everybody. We've got a gigantic innertube. It's really fun. Ten people can ride on it, and it spins."

"I already told AJ that I was working every day this week."

"Just come over after you get off. I'll go out on the water with y'all."

"But your leg."

"I'll live."

"I would, but I don't want to try to act like I don't know you in front of him again. That's just weird. I'm definitely closer to you than I am to AJ."

"Well, I hope so," he said, reaching out for my hand. "Why don't we just go ahead and tell him. If we tell AJ we're together, then there's no confusion, and you can just come over there and be there with me."

"We would never tell AJ we're together," I said, half-thinking he was joking.

"Why not?"

"Because then we would basically be telling the whole family."

"Yeah?"

I looked at him like he must know he was missing something. "That's not what this is, though," I said.

"What do you mean that's not what this is?" he asked.

"Well, me and AJ were hanging out, but we never had any future plans or made any kind of announcement or anything. No one really even knew I was there to hang out with him. It's casual."

Charlie's eyebrows furrowed when I said that. "Casual? You're saying whatever's going on between me and you, it's too casual for me to say anything about it to AJ or my family? Is that how you feel?"

"I thought that's just how it was," I said, feeling somewhat stunned.

"Are you embarrassed?"

"What? Embarrassed? Me of you? No. Why would I be?"

"You tell me. You're the one who doesn't want to tell my family you're coming over to see me."

"I didn't say that, I just said we shouldn't make any announcements about it. AJ's going back to Chicago, and you're going back to Miami. There are too many factors for you to go mentioning this to anyone, that's all."

"What are these factors?" Charlie asked, pulling back and looking confused.

I put a hand to my chest, hesitating and feeling at a loss of words. My mouth was suddenly dry, but I continued. "I don't want a lasting relationship, and you certainly aren't ready for one, so ultimately this thing that's going on between us is kind of a temporary thing, you know? I'm so sorry to say it like that, but that's what I assumed. That's really what it boils down to. It's temporary with these vacation things. That's why they're called flings."

"Is that what you think is going on here?"

"Yes. It is what's going on here."

"Well, that's news to me because that's not how it feels with me."

"Yes, it is. It's got to be. You're less ready for a relationship than I am, Charlie. And it's not just that. There are factors with my dad and the whole thing with Savannah. We're probably doing the wrong thing by even letting it go this far. But it's like… once I kiss you it's like the most wonderful thing I've ever done, and I just get all carried away."

I was being lighthearted, but Charlie just looked at me with that same serious, confused expression. "What's going on with your dad and Savannah?" he asked. "What do they have to do with us?"

"They have everything to do with us. Everything to do with the fact that this thing we're doing is temporary."

"Enlighten me, Hope. Tell me why it's temporary."

"My dad is a doo-something with y'all. Ms. Bridgette was telling me. It's a Bible word—it's Greek I think. It means a slave. It's a thing in the Bible where someone is a slave and then they don't have to be one anymore, but they go back to it because slavery in the nice house is better than their other life."

Charlie stared blankly at me." I'm sorry but what in the world are you talking about, Hope?"

"It's a Greek word. It's what my dad is doing."

"Are you saying that the fact that your dad works for my dad is preventing you from being with me?"

"You say *being with me* like that's what we're doing here. You make it sound like you think it's long-term or something."

"I'm glad I make it seem like that, because that is what I think. This is long-term to me."

"Charlie."

"What?"

"Don't," I said.

"Don't what?"

"Don't tease me."

"Seriously, what are you saying? Your dad works for us. It's a regular job. A good job. Do you think it's a problem?"

My heart started beating a thousand miles an hour because I knew I just needed to come out and say the other thing. "Charlie, I'll never forget Savannah."

He let out a scoffing sound that was a result of being at a loss for words. "I won't either," he said.

"Exactly," I said. "I'm going to be honest with you. I had a crush on you for years of my life—probably a decade. I was super excited when I heard you were back in town, and then the instant I found out you were married, I flipped a switch. And then I loved her. I got to know her, and she was beautiful and amazing, and I knew I would never love or marry someone who's already been married, especially to someone like her. So, I just turned all my feelings off toward you because I knew it would never happen."

Even as I let the sentence come out of my mouth I knew I was misrepresenting myself and my feelings. I knew he would take this the wrong way. He had taken it the wrong way. I could tell by his facial expression. He had been hurt. He was scowling.

"So, basically you're saying I'm unlovable now because I've been married before?"

"You're, no. No way. You're definitely lovable, Charlie. You're extremely lovable."

"Just not by you?"

I stared at him feeling completely taken off guard. My heart was racing and I felt like he thought I was breaking up with him even though we were never together.

"You don't need me to love you," I said. "You have a whole life in Florida that you're forgetting about."

"I'm not forgetting about it, I'm just telling you I want you in it."

"In what? Your life?" I asked.

"Yes."

"Charlie, you have no idea what you're saying. Honestly, my body goes completely haywire from you saying that. I seriously feel like my heart might jump out of my chest when you look at me—let alone when you touch me. I am so attracted to you I can hardly breathe. But I can't think ahead to futuristic things with you. I know I wouldn't be able to be with you in deeper ways and then think about you being with her."

"So, you wouldn't be able to be with anybody who's ever been with someone?"

I could feel tears start to fill my eyes because I didn't know how to explain myself. I could see that his feelings were hurt.

"I want to be with you. When I'm with you, I get all caught up in these feelings like I could. But you were married, Charlie. The whole reason you're in Arkansas is because you're so devastated by losing her that you can't live a normal life."

"What if I don't want to go back to my normal life? What if it's like you were saying about your dad? What if my life is better here?"

"You're saying that because you're here with me and that's all you're thinking about, but you wouldn't feel that way if you went back to Miami. I wasn't your first choice last year when Savannah was here with you. There's no reason I should be your first choice now."

"Of course, I'm not going to look at you back then, Hope, because I was with someone else."

"That's what I'm saying, Charlie, you need to find someone who didn't know Savannah. You need to find someone who wasn't rejected by you already."

He put his hands on his head and stretched upward it was a frustrated gesture like he was trying to remain patient.

"So, you're just messing around with me?" he asked. "Anything that happens between us doesn't mean anything to you, and you're just messing around?"

I stared at him, blinking. "You're the one who's not thinking clearly right now, Charlie. It's you who this stuff doesn't mean anything to. I'm just trying to remind you of that."

"I'm the one who knows what I feel. I'm the one who's sitting here saying I love you and I want to be with you."

"No, you don't love me Charlie. Not ultimately."

He looked me in the eyes with a serious expression. "I'm doing my best to not get frustrated right now, Hope. But you're talking in circles. If you don't want to be with me, just come out and say it."

"It's not that easy because technically I do want to be with you. My body is on fire right now, and I feel out of control because I physically want to hold you and touch you."

"But what?" he asked when I hesitated.

"But Charlie. Everything. Her. I'm not gonna be able to get over thinking about you thinking about her. I'm always going to think you're sad and you still miss her."

"What if I tell you that's false? That you're wrong. Is it not good enough for me to tell you that? It boils down to trust, Hope. You have to trust me, and right now you don't."

"I trust you as a person. I know you're a great person. I was just never under the assumption that this would ever lead to anything. I knew it wouldn't."

"It sounds like the bottom line is that you don't want me."

"It's not that simple. I am not good enough for you, Charlie, and right now you think I am because you're here and you're broken. The minute you get back to the real world you're not going to want this anymore. I already know that because you didn't choose me once before."

Charlie stayed quiet for a while, shaking his head slightly like he was in deep thought.

"I can't tell what you're doing, Hope. You're saying I didn't choose you before, and maybe that's the truth to some extent, but I was already with her when I came here."

"I know that, Charlie. And I'm not trying to punish you for being married to someone else. I just never saw that as my fate—being with someone who's been married. And it's not like you wanted her to be gone. You still loved her. She was taken from you when you still loved her."

"Exactly, which is why it's unbelievable that it's happening again."

I started to say something to respond to him and then I realized I didn't have a response. I felt so shocked that I stuttered for a second as I smiled. "Th-wh-I love you too, but let's face it. We love each other as humans and we'd do anything for each other, but you don't *love me* love me. I'm not like Savannah, Charlie, and I definitely don't want to think about you comparing me to her about marital things."

He made an offended face, staring at me. "You're just assuming you know what's in my head. Do you assume that I'm sitting there comparing you to Savannah every time we're together?"

"No, honestly, because I don't even think of myself as making it that far in your thoughts. Right now, this, what we're doing, I don't struggle with it at all."

He let out a humorless laugh.

"What?" I asked.

"You're being mean. You're saying you're okay with messing around with my feelings."

"No, I'm saying I'm okay with you messing around with mine," I said. Hot tears overflowed my eyes and spilled out onto my cheeks. I was wound up, and I felt mad that he was teasing me about something I had wanted for so long and had finally gotten over.

Charlie could see that I was now serious and upset, and he stared at me, looking me over intently and trying to figure out what to say. He took a deep breath and made a face like he was about to say something but then stopped himself. Finally, he spoke.

"Hope, I can't tell what you want, so I am going to leave you alone. You obviously need to figure out some things on your own." He put a hand to his chest. "As for me, I want you. These last few days apart from you only confirmed that. But I want to be with you in ways that you don't want to be with me. That's something I can't change. I can't change what happened with Savannah or the fact that I married her. That whole thing is just part of who I am now. If you can't bring yourself to love me as the man I am now, then there's nothing I can do about it."

He stood up.

"Are you leaving?"

"Yes. What else can I do? If you'll tell me something I can do to earn your trust or make you love me, I'll do it."

I sat on the couch and he looked down at me, waiting for my answer. My cheeks were tear-soaked and I stared up at him as hopelessly as I felt.

I didn't know what to say.

I couldn't think of anything he could do, shy of becoming a time traveler.

Chapter 16

I watched Charlie walk out of my apartment, and I did nothing to stop him.

He walked away, and I sat on the couch and watched him do it.

I felt absolutely crushed.

I was broken and spilled out. I felt stunned, petrified, like my feet had turned to cement and I couldn't move off of that place on the couch. Charlie walked out of my apartment, and I sat there like a stone statue and let him.

It was quiet in my apartment, and I heard his truck as he drove off.

I cried. Silent, hot tears ran down my cheeks in continual streams.

It was all too much. I had assumed this whole time that Charlie did not want me that way. I did not imagine that my life would ever be able to connect with his in that capacity.

I was terrified at the thought of living with another woman's memory, but I was more terrified of losing Charlie.

He had left, and I felt a crushing void because of it. It was as if I needed to have him back in order to breathe. I was devastated without him. This feeling was worse than any of the fears I had about being with him.

I was actively shedding tears when I called Charlie on the phone. Tears were rolling out of my eyes and my breath hitched continually. Charlie's phone rang four times before going to voicemail, and I cried some more.

I went to my window and looked out of it. He had already left, and I did what I had to do. I went after him. I grabbed my purse, phone, and keys, and just like that, with wet hair and sweatpants, I took off in my car, headed to Broken Arrow, Arkansas.

I drove south toward State Road 25, and once I had settled down a little bit, I called Charlie again. I figured if I drove quickly, I would catch up to him within a couple of minutes at the most. The phone rang four times and then went to his voicemail again.

I had hardly stopped crying. Silent tears ran down my swollen, burning face. I hung up, and seconds later, Charlie called me back, thank goodness.

I held the phone to my ear, blinking away tears as I drove down quiet, familiar roads.

"Hey," I said, trying to control my shaking weak voice.

"Hey," he said. "My phone was on silent. I just saw you called."

"Hey, where are you? I'm on the road right behind you."

"Nobody's right behind me," he said.

"Yeah, but I must be close. How far are you?"

"How far from what?" he said.

"My house. Aren't you headed back home?"

"No. I'm not paying attention to directions right now. I was going to drive around for a while."

"Did you leave in the same direction you came?" I asked. My voice still shook, but I did my best.

"No, I did not go that way. I think I'm by the road that leads to Sandy Beach. I see the sign for it right here."

"Sandy Beach? Why did you go that way?"

"Why are you calling me?"

"I need you to please wait where you are, Charlie, because I have to talk to you. I'm turning around now. I'm in the car, and I have to turn around, hang on. I thought I followed you. Are you for sure at Sandy Beach? Can you just wait there? Do you remember where we went before?" My words came out quickly in spite of my voice being shaky and quiet.

"Yes, I remember where we went before. I see that same parking lot right now."

"Why'd you go that way? Please park and wait there. I'm on my way. It's going to be like three or five minutes. Will you stay there?"

"Yes, I will."

I hung up with Charlie.

I knew he would be waiting there for me, and I felt an ember of hope in the midst of all the wretched, hopeless feelings.

I parked right next to Charlie's truck and got out, looking inside, trying to see if he was sitting in there.

I heard him whistle from the beach, and I ran to him instantly.

I didn't take my keys or my phone. I left it all in the car. I didn't care.

I saw Charlie in the distance. The sun had gone down, and we were now operating in moonlight. The lake was behind him and we walked toward each other with long strides. I wasn't bawling like a baby, but there was nothing I could do to stop the flow of liquid that came out of my eyes. I tucked my head as I approached him because I didn't want him to see me crying.

Charlie took me into his strong embrace with no hesitation. He saw that I wanted to go to him, and he took me in, wrapping his arms around me, enveloping me with warmth and hard muscle. I rested my head on his chest and took a deep breath. I gasped a little, but I tried to make myself stop.

I didn't even realize how tightly I had been holding onto him until he rubbed my back and caused me to relax.

"Charlie, I-I didn't want you to leave," I said, trying my very best not to cry. "I don't know what I said that made you go so fast... I mean, I understand, but I didn't expect you to say you ever wanted me like that... I didn't ever consider that you might be ready for a..." I took a second to take a deep breath. I rested the side of my head on his chest and covered my face with my hand. "Charlie I still feel scared when I think about trying to start something with you, but I feel way, way, way more afraid of you driving off and being out of my life. I felt horrible just now." He held me tightly and took a deep breath like he was about to reply. But I started speaking again. "I should have said I love you back when you said it. I should have told you that I was just too scared to love you but that deep down I really do. All that stuff I was talking about, that's just me being afraid. I don't know what you're trying to have with me, Charlie, but I want it whatever it is. I'm sorry I said otherwise." I took a long, deep, hitching breath in and held him, molding my body to his. "I'm sorry," I whispered. My arms were wrapped tightly around his midsection, and my hands rested on his sides. I could feel his hard, tone, substantial body under the thin layer of t-shirt, and I ached with the need to be near him. "I'm sorry I said I can't forget her," I whispered. "You are who you are, and it's up to me to get over it. I know I can get over it. You just surprised me with everything you were saying, and I said the first thing that came to my mind."

"I shouldn't have left," he said. "I didn't know what to do, either. I freaked out. I was already thinking about going back. That's why I drove over here. I was staying in town."

Charlie held me tightly, and I felt sweet relief at his words and affection.

"Hope, I don't compare you to anyone, and I don't think anything about your dad working for my dad. Those things are so far from my mind that it's shocking to me that they would hold you back from being with me."

"It's shocking to me that you want to talk about this in front of your family."

"If you're embarrassed, we definitely don't have to say anything."

"I'm not embarrassed," I said, holding onto him and not looking at him. "Why would I be embarrassed? I'm embarrassed for you." I added that last part humbly because it was the truth. Deep down, I truly did not believe that I was good enough for him. That was what this was all about.

But I had to get over it, or I would lose him.

He said he loved me, and he was holding me like he wanted me, and that would have to be good enough to get me through this insecurity.

He took a deep breath, and his whole body expanded. I smiled at the feel of his hard, ribbed muscles tensing under my arms. He began moving back, and I realized he had ducked and was trying to get me to look at him. My eyes met his for the first time since we connected on the beach.

I had been crying, and I knew it was obvious, but I let my eyes meet his. I smiled past the burning sensation in my face.

"What do you mean you're embarrassed for me?"

"Nothing actually," I said with a self-deprecating sigh. "I shouldn't have said that. That's my the-world-is-falling-apart mode. I know it's not the truth."

"I'm not sure if you think I don't deserve you or you don't deserve me, but neither are true. Both of us need to be clear on that."

I nodded "I am. I know." I blinked at him. "I was really sad just now when you left," I said softly, shyly, flirting with him a little.

I did not have to flirt twice. Charlie's lips were on mine before I knew what was happening. I felt the warm, wet intrusion of his tongue almost instantly, and I leaned into him, holding him closer, letting my body shape to his.

He pulled back too soon. "Please don't do that again," he whispered.

He kissed me deeply again after he said that. It was another quick, soft, amazing intrusion and then he broke contact again.

"Okay," I agreed. "I won't." I took another deep breath, and I gasped lightly a few times.

He grinned slowly at me, and I bit my lip, staring at him. A few others were out on the beach, but there was plenty of room and none of us were in earshot of each other.

"Next time, don't run off so fast," I said to Charlie. "All of a sudden you were gone, and I felt like my bones were broken."

"Your bones?" he asked, his chest shaking with laughter. "I'm sorry for leaving," he said. "I would've come back if you didn't call." He gave me a long squeeze, holding me close to him, hugging me. "I wanted you to want me so bad," he said. "I knew rejection was a possibility, but I came over here thinking it would all work out."

"It will work out. It can work out. It just took me a second. I'm still scared to death, honestly. I'm not even sure I know what you're asking me. Are you talking about us being officially more than friends?"

He smiled and ducked to kiss me again. He let his mouth gently touch mine, and then pulled back just far enough to barely break contact.

"Yes, I'm talking about being more than friends, Hope. I don't want to be your friend anymore. I understand if you're not comfortable with coming over right away with AJ, but I don't want to hide it. I think our parents should definitely know. It's going to affect my plans or your plans… some of our plans will have to change."

"Are you referring to the fact that you're going back to Miami after summer?"

"Yes."

"I know. That's coming soon."

I leaned up and kissed his cheek after I said that. Our faces were still really close to each other, and it took no effort at all for me to stretch up and close the small gap. He squeezed me and leaned in, holding me there.

"It's coming too soon," he said. "And, I'm not looking forward to leaving you here, so we need to be thinking about what we're going to do."

I reached up and touched the side of his face. "That's hard because both of us have to work. You need to get back to Miami for your work, and I won't have work if I leave here."

"Just say you'll stay with me, and we can worry about the rest later," he said softly.

"I'll stay with you." I touched the side of his face again. I let my fingertips run across his hairline at his temple, marveling at how I loved everything about him. I felt electrical shocks in my fingertips as a result of touching his skin, and I smiled because of it. "I'll follow you, Charlie, wherever you ask me to go."

Chapter 17

Charlie Morgan

The following day

"Don't be mad at me, Maximus."

Charlie shook his head at his brother, Casey, as he drove. "You told me it was right down the street, and we were halfway to Little Rock."

"It was twenty minutes, tops."

"Yeah, but that was an hour ago. How do you already have access to that place if you haven't bought it yet?"

"Why are you in such a hurry to get back to the house?" Casey asked, ignoring the other question.

"Because Hope is already over there. She took off early and said she'd be at the house by four. What are you doing buying a house out here in the middle of nowhere, anyway?"

Casey didn't answer.

Charlie didn't usually ask Casey or his father about the odd things they did with their work. He honestly didn't want to know. They had work colleagues who they would entertain and travel with, and Charlie figured this house in the middle of nowhere Arkansas was part of that. He didn't know every detail about their work, but he knew they were good men. They weren't into anything immoral in spite of a few rumors. He didn't talk to anyone about their dad's house in the woods, and he wouldn't tell anyone about Casey's new real estate venture. He knew that his dad and brother talked to each other about all of that, but he didn't mention their business to anyone.

"It's just a rental. I would have just borrowed your truck instead of you driving, but you said you'd give me a ride."

"I didn't mind giving you a ride. But that's when I thought it was right down the road," Charlie said.

"Since when are you freaking out to see AJ's girlfriend?" Casey laughed and covered his mouth with his fist when he said it, watching and waiting for Charlie's reaction.

Charlie knew his brother was saying that to try to get a rise out of him. He had succeeded. Charlie's blood pressure was through the roof as a result of that comment.

"I know you're just joking and everything, but I seriously never ever want you to call her that again."

Casey laughed and covered his mouth even more, teasing Charlie for being so wound up about it. Charlie smiled a little and shook his head.

"You laugh, but I'm protective of her. Please don't say any of this in front of her or AJ. It would make her uncomfortable."

"I didn't know you were that serious about her."

"I am so serious. I saw my future running toward me in the sand in a pair of fuzzy socks last night."

"What do you mean?" Casey asked, laughing.

"She chased me down at that beach in Graham Springs last night and she ran through the sand in these big fluffy socks. She drove in them."

"She drove in socks?"

"Yeah, and then trudged through the sand in them. I stood there with her for a half-hour before I brought it up and we laughed about it. I looked down at those socks in the sand, and I realized I was going to be old with this woman."

"You have got to be kidding me. How can something like this happen twice to one guy? Are you just good at falling in love or something?"

"I don't know. I don't think I am. I wasn't trying to fall in love. I didn't come here for that. Even last night, I told myself I should leave her alone, but I just couldn't. If anything, I'm trying to hold myself back from falling in love so soon. I don't want to make myself susceptible to that type of heartbreak again. But I just couldn't let her go. I couldn't get her out of my mind. I know you've heard me say this before, and it's unbelievable, even to me, that I'm saying it again. But I love her. That's why I don't want her over there with AJ right now."

"You should just tell AJ the truth if you love her so much."

"I would, in a heartbeat, but Hope doesn't want to yet, and I understand. AJ and Aunt Astrid are only going to be at the house for a couple more days, so we're going to be neutral in front of everyone and not make it weird. That's why I'm telling you about all this though. If you see me trying to sneak around with Hope, don't call us out. Tell dad, too. Just stay neutral till the Camerons leave."

"And then what happens when they come back for Christmas they just see y'all married?"

"They probably will," Charlie said. "And we'll deal with it then."

"You're seriously unbelievable," Casey replied, shaking his head.

"I assure you I did not try to let this happen," Charlie said. "But if I don't snatch her up, someone else will, and I'll never forgive myself if I let that happen. She drug me out of that hole I was in, Casey. I need her."

"Yeah, are you sure that's not the reason? Maybe she was at the right place at the right time."

"I get what you're saying, and I knew people would think that. It's what I expected after finding her so quickly. But no. It's not a rebound situation. We were just friends for months. And, besides, I just want to be with her. I want to spend time with her. She's beautiful, and fun, and funny, and she laughs at all my jokes. I'm looking forward to seeing her right now. I'm sad that she's there and I'm not."

"AJ's going to know something's going on with you acting all lovestruck like that."

"I'm not going to mention any of this to AJ. But I'm fine if he knows, I'm just trying to be considerate."

"Did you ever consider staying single for a year or two, Charlie?" Casey asked in the way only a brother could.

Charlie knew Casey didn't mean any harm. He was surprised that was all he had to say. "Not really," Charlie said as he shrugged and smiled at his brother.

He turned up the truck radio.

The two of them listened to music in silence for a few minutes, and then they went back and forth from quiet to talking until they arrived back at the house. Hope's car was in the driveway, and Charlie felt like he might burst if he didn't make it inside to see her.

The house was so big that people didn't usually keep up with other people's comings and goings. Casey went in using another door, and Charlie went in search of Hope. There were several people in the living room when he got back, and they all noticed when he walked in. Hope was nowhere in sight. It looked like everyone was playing a game around the dinner table, and they stopped and greeted Charlie.

"Hope was supposed to come over," he said.

He told himself to play it cool. He had been trying not to make it the first thing he said when he walked in, but the words just came out of his mouth.

"Oh, she got roped into going out on the boat with my crew," Astrid said. "Beau had everybody trying to climb that big cliff face at the bottom of Michael Simon's property today."

"Are you talking about Hope?" Max asked.

Charlie turned to find his dad who is just walking into the room. "Yes, Hope," Charlie said to him.

"Hope got talked into going out to Michael's Bluff for a little while. I know where they are. I could take you over there if you want to go meet them."

Charlie agreed casually, but he sprang into action, and it only took him three minutes to get down to the dock and ready to go. He saw his dad coming out to meet him.

"I'll just take the boat over there," Charlie said when Max came near. "I think I know where that bluff is. Is it that big one past the white house?"

Max nodded and kept on approaching. "Yeah, I was up at the house talking to Hope when they asked her to go. Beau and AJ had come back to get stuff for the ice chest, and they got to talking about that rock wall and her climbing skills. Of course, Beau had to challenge her."

"She doesn't even climb real rocks," Charlie said.

"Yeah, but you know that one they're going to. She said she's climbed that one before. I can even climb that one." Max stopped in his tracks. "I'll just go back up to the house since you know where you're going, though. Are you sure you've got it with your leg?"

"Yeah, it's no problem." Charlie didn't even feel his leg. It was still aching, but he didn't care. He already had swim trunks on and was prepared to go climbing or swimming if he had to.

"She looked at me as she left, and she smiled at me," Max said.

"What's that supposed to mean?" Charlie asked, looking at his father for the odd comment.

Max shrugged. "I don't know, she smiled at me, and I knew it was about you, that's all."

***

It took ten minutes of boating to make it to the right place. Charlie saw a few different boats at the spot, but he easily found his cousins and their friends from Chicago on his dad's big boat. Danny Cameron, Astrid's husband, was obviously captaining because he stood behind the helm. AJ and some others were on the boat as well. But Hope and one of the girls from Chicago were up on top of the small cliff. Hope had on short-shorts with a one-piece swimsuit as a shirt. She was soaking wet and had been in the water, and she started smiling and waving as soon as she caught sight of Charlie.

He waved back at her, and she held her nose and jumped into the lake in a comfortable position feet-first like she was seated in a recliner. She had chosen a good spot and jumped in at a reasonable trajectory, but Charlie watched her, feeling his heart stop as he waited for her to surface. He wanted to jump in and swim to her. There was nothing he could do to stop his mind from flashing to Savannah, but for Hope's sake he didn't want his fears to control him. He hated to think of the possibility of ever losing Hope, though, and he ached to protect her.

He breathed again once her head popped out of the water. She was wearing a smile and Charlie took a deep, calming breath. He wondered if any of this would ever get easier. He had to think it would. He had to let go and live life and trust that those he loved would be okay.

Hope was obviously fine. She was having fun. She swam toward Charlie who had now coasted to the waters closer to her. Hope was about halfway to him when she turned around in the water and waved at the girl who was still standing on the cliff.

"Jump right where I did," she yelled. "It's deep. I went down far, and I didn't touch anything."

She turned and started swimming toward Charlie's boat again. He smiled as he watched her. He came to the side of the boat as she swam to him.

"Sophia was afraid she was going to hit bottom, so I was up there showing her where to jump." There was a small ladder on the back of the boat, and Hope climbed onto it as she spoke. "Hey, Charlie," she continued, climbing out of the water.

Charlie moved to her, helping her up. "Hey, Hope."

"I'm glad you're here. I left something at the house," she said. "Would you mind taking me back there real quick?"

"Sure. Of course."

She stood up to her full height and they balanced on the small boat. They were only a foot or two apart, and she smiled at him. "Take me over there to the big boat, if you don't mind, so I can tell them what we're doing."

Within a minute, they had made their way close enough to the big boat that they could speak and be heard without yelling.

"I forgot something at the house and Charlie's going to take me back there to get it. Do you guys need anything?"

A few of them shook their head like they didn't need anything but Beau yelled out. "If your leg wasn't hurt, you would have to race Hope up that cliff. She's amazing."

Hope looked at Charlie. "He took it easy on me," she whispered. "He's just trying to talk the girls into doing it. They walk around the trail to get to the top. It takes fifteen minutes."

Just then, Sophia (who hadn't heard any of that) shrieked and jumped off of the small cliff and into the water. Hope cheered for her when she came up, and the boat swayed, causing Hope to flinch in order to steady herself. She grabbed Charlie's arm to do it, and his chest felt tight.

Chapter 18

Hope Jones

I forgot to take my allergy medicine.

It was a stretch of an excuse since, technically, I could go without taking it. But I hadn't taken it that day, and I did have some of it back at the house, so it was as close as I could come to a legit excuse when I only wanted to be alone with Charlie. I was usually not very good at lying, but I had to say something. I hated that I was gone when he got back to the house, and I was so happy to see him coming out there on the boat alone. I jumped off of the cliff even though Sophia wasn't ready for me to, and I swam straight to his boat instead of the boat I had gone there on.

Sophia eventually jumped and I yelled out to cheer for her which made me shake the boat.

"I'm sorry," I said, steadying myself on Charlie's arm. He looked straight at me when I said that, and our eyes locked in spite of the fact that he had on sunglasses. They were transparent enough and it was bright enough outside for me to see his eyes. We were shouting distance from the Morgan's other boat and there were several other boats around—otherwise I would have hugged him, kissed him, and greeted him like I wanted to. He had come there for me, and I was relieved to see him.

Last night had been so surreal that I doubted myself and wondered if it had all been a dream. But now that Charlie was here and we were together, I knew it was a reality. Charlie was my new reality. AJ yelled something, and it took me a second to figure out that he was talking to us.

"I will!" Charlie yelled, speaking to AJ. He looked that way, smiling and waving easily. "If she wants to come back," Charlie added, yelling and smiling at his cousin as he moved toward his place near the back of the boat.

"What'd he say?" I asked, quietly, as I moved back there with him.

"He said for me not to forget to bring you back."

"You can do whatever you want," I said. I smiled at him like it was a casual statement, but I was serious.

There was room for four in the boat. Two single seats were both available, but I took the fourth seat, which was a shared bench seat with the captain. I got settled next to Charlie, not caring if anyone in the other boat noticed or cared about our seating arrangements. I figured it was logical that I would sit next to him even if I wasn't in love with him, though.

Charlie took off, pulling away from the bluff and heading toward the Morgan mansion.

It only took a minute for us to travel far enough to make it out of view from the others. I turned and looked over my shoulder to make sure no one could see us, and then I reached out to hold Charlie's hand. He held the steering wheel with one hand and grabbed me with the other. He brought my hand up to his mouth and kissed it.

"I missed you," I said, speaking loudly over the sound of the boat motor.

"I missed you," he said. He held my hand close to his chest as he navigated the waters. "Did you really forget something at the house?"

"No," I said easily, assuming he knew. "I was thinking of an allergy pill, but it was a fake excuse."

He looked at me and grinned. "I was hoping you would say that," he said.

I turned and rested my head on his shoulder, looking out at the lake as we made our way toward the house. We rode in silence for a minute while Charlie held onto my hand. I was focused on the sensation of it all—the wind on my face and the feeling of his hand around mine.

"Did you beat my cousins climbing up that rock?" he asked.

"We were just messing around," I said. "We were trying to get those Chicago girls to climb up there and jump in. It was fun, though. I live on this lake, and I go out and swim, but I never go climbing."

"I know. You use Landon's plastic rocks instead."

"Yeah, even Landon has been trying to get me to climb real rocks."

I heard the boat motor change in pitch and I felt the boat suddenly slow down as Charlie adjusted the throttle. We came to an almost instant stop, and I laughed and held onto him as we leaned forward. He regarded me with an easy half-smile when I turned to stare at him.

"Why'd you stop?" I asked. We were still a mile from the house, and I looked around, wondering what I missed.

"Landon," he said, shaking his head. "I don't mean to let it bug me that you spend so much time alone with Landon. I know he's your friend."

I leaned in and kissed Charlie. He was precious. I had done a ton of thinking since I saw him last, and all of it led to one answer. I loved Charlie Morgan with all my heart. I loved the crooked broken road he took to get to me, and I loved the man he was because of the journey he had taken down that road. I also loved that he was jealous. I wanted him to be boat-stoppingly jealous of me, and I kissed him because of it. I kissed his mouth several times softly before pulling back and smiling at him. I couldn't help but smile. He was so perfect and handsome that I smiled just being near him. I couldn't believe I was sitting there, on a boat, touching and kissing him at my own discretion.

"You're really right though," I said. "I wouldn't love it if you had a female friend who you always spent time with—even if it was innocent. That would still be kind of annoying to me. I'll have Stacy go over there with me, or I'll figure something out where she's with us most of the time when we're hanging out. She likes him, anyway. I know she'd want to go over there with me."

"You don't have to make special arrangements," he said. "I hate you being over there with him, but I trust you." He shrugged. "I was mostly just stopping the boat to get a second alone with you."

"I haven't stopped thinking about you all day," I said. "I thought about what you said last night and how I reacted, and I'm so sorry. I should have told you that you're my biggest crush, Charlie. You're my dream guy. Just looking at you makes my heart… here, feel it." I took his hand and rested his fingertips just under my jaw in the sensitive flesh that I knew was vulnerable and pulsing. He rested his fingertips there for a few seconds and then I looked at him, wondering if he felt it.

"I can't feel anything for the pounding of my own heart, Hope. I'm just leaving my hand there because I like touching your neck."

I brought his hand up to my mouth and kissed the backside of his fingers, letting his hand linger on my closed mouth. "I wanted you to know that I so regretted how I reacted last night."

"I figured that out when you chased me across town in your socks."

"I know. And I'm glad I did that, but last night when I was lying in bed, I was just thinking about everything, and I really wish I would've reacted differently."

"I don't know," he said, tilting his head at me. "I get what you're saying. I have things I wish I would've done differently too, but all of those things led us here. Last night, with the beach and the socks, it was so perfect. Even if it took you rejecting me first—I wouldn't trade that sight of you in the sand for anything."

I leaned in and kissed him when he said that, and he smiled as I broke away.

"I want to do the opposite of reject you," I said. "Is a kiss the opposite of that?" I asked the question with furrowed eyebrows as if I was serious and then I leaned in and did it again. "I'm the opposite of rejecting you right now," I said. I did it again after that just to make sure.

I had been looking at Charlie's face for months, but now I saw him differently, and it made my gut ache. I was crushing on him harder than ever, and it was unbelievable to me that he felt the same way. I sat back, playing it cool, holding his hand and assuming he would take off again, which he did.

We held hands all the way back to the house. I adjusted in my seat and let go of him when I saw a couple of people waiting outside. It was Casey and their Aunt Astrid, and I scooted slightly further from Charlie.

They were on the dock, and they walked toward the end of it to meet us when we drifted up.

"I'm going back with y'all," Casey called as we came closer. "I wish I would have known you were going a minute ago. I would have gone with you."

"How'd you know we were coming back?"

"Beau called to tell me to ride back with you. He said they were out at that cliff."

"I'm not going back with you," Astrid said, holding up a backpack. "My husband called and said for me to send his camera back with you."

Charlie moved to the edge of the boat and Astrid handed him a bag.

"Be careful, there's expensive stuff in there."

"Why did you come back?" Casey asked, looking at us as if making sure we were okay.

"I'm running up to the house to take my allergy medicine," I said, raising my hand a little. I waited until Charlie was done with the camera bag exchange and then I got off of the boat carefully, standing on the dock near Astrid. I looked at Casey. "I know you're waiting on us to take you back, so I won't be long," I said. My gaze shifted to Charlie. "Do you need anything from the house while I'm up there?"

"No, thank you," he said.

"Okay, I'll be back," I said. I turned and began jogging up the dock, leaving everyone else down there without looking back.

Chapter 19

I had left my allergy medicine in my purse, which was in the house. I spoke to a couple of people in the kitchen while I was in there, but I moved quickly since I knew they were waiting. I took the small pill with a sip of water and then I went to use the restroom.

I kept replaying moments in my head. They all boiled down to one thing:

I loved Charlie.

A smile spread across my face at the thought of him. I remembered holding his hand on the boat and the way he stopped it in the middle of the lake. My mind was in another location as I went through the motions in the restroom—flush, wash my hands, dry my hands, open the door, turn off the light…

"Oh, Mister Max, you scared me."

"I do that to people," he said, smiling at me from the hallway.

"I was just headed outside." I looked him over. At first, I thought he might've been in line for the restroom, but there were ten other restrooms in this house, and he was standing there looking at me, so I figured he had something to say. My face grew serious and I stared at him feeling a little worried. "Is everything okay?"

"Yes, it is. I saw you come in here, and I just wanted to try to catch you alone for a second and thank you."

"No problem at all. It was just some envelopes. My dad called me before I even left Graham Springs, and I just stopped at the store on my way out."

"I'm not talking about envelopes. I didn't even know you brought anything over here."

"Oh, yeah I'm sorry. He said it was for some package you were mailing so I thought…"

"He is mailing that for me. I didn't know he called you to pick up envelopes. Thank you for doing that. No, I wanted to thank you for something else. Something more significant than office supplies."

"What is it?" I asked, looking at him curiously.

Max reached out, took me into his arms, and hugged me. I liked Max Morgan a lot. I had good conversations with him over the years. But never in any of our encounters had he just walked up to me and wrapped his arms around me. He wasn't someone I would categorize as a tender guy, and I wasn't quite sure what to make of this hug. I stood there for several long seconds and when he didn't let go, I patted his back a few times.

"I thought I had lost him for good," Max said still holding me. He let go, pulling me back and looking me in the eyes. "I'm not talking about just losing him by him staying here in Arkansas. I knew it was a possibility that he would leave Miami, and I had come to terms with that. But I thought that guilt might actually kill him." He stared at me seriously. "Your name says it all… you brought literal hope. I had been calling him every night because I was worried about him. He was different—closed off—a shell of the person he used to be. He had sold some things in Miami, and quite frankly I thought he might… I thought I might lose him. He was lost. For a while there, he was lost. And it got me praying. I prayed to God every day, literally on my knees. I was talking to God more during that time than I have the whole rest of my life combined. I probably shouldn't admit that. But I felt helpless for my son, and it was all I knew to do. Then I remember this one night I talked to Charlie and his voice sounded different. There was life in his voice, and he told me he found Hope in the woods." Max smiled. "I knew he was talking about you because he clarified by saying Paul's daughter, but I also knew that you had delivered the other kind of hope—the kind I had been praying for." Max smiled and paused. "It's just sweet that God would pick someone who's actually named that," he said with a little laugh. "I just think that's such a nice touch on God's part."

Max was so sincere that I felt undeserving. "Wow, goodness, thank you Mr. Max. I love spending time with Charlie. If anything, he helps me out."

He smiled and drew me into his arms again. "And I think he likes you," he said as he let me go. "I know you came here to visit with AJ, and I'm not trying to—"

"I'm definitely here to see Charlie," I said in an easy tone that reflected how convinced I was.

Max grinned at me but then shook his head. "Well, you probably need to get back on the water if you're here to see Charlie. He left a little while ago in the small boat, looking for you."

"Oh, I found Charlie. He gave me a ride back, and now he's down at the dock. We're in the small boat together."

"Oh, good, so you've already found him."

"Yes sir, I found him," I assured Max. I invited him to go back to Michael's Bluff with us, but he didn't end up going. He stayed back at the house, and I thought about what he said as I walked outside and back down to the lake.

Both of the guys were waiting on the boat, and I moved quickly to get to them. They were standing up and looking like a handsome pair—like some kind of commercial.

They moved to find their places as I made it to the end of the dock and approached the side of the boat. Casey had already moved to the single seat that was positioned in the front of the boat and he stepped forward to give me a hand to steady myself. I took his hand even though I was accustomed to stepping onto boats.

"My brother likes you, Hope Jones."

"Does he?" I said. A smile covered my face. There was nothing I could do to remove it. "I like your brother back," I said, trying to be lighthearted even though my heart was pounding.

"That's why I let you sit back there on the bench seat."

"Oh, *you* let her sit back here?" Charlie asked, messing around.

I smiled at them and started making my way to the back of the boat to meet up with Charlie. It was just a few steps, but I walked carefully on the shifting surface. Charlie stuck his hand out to help me as I got closer to him.

"I did you a favor, brother," Casey said to him. "It's better to just come out and say it if you like someone."

I turned and looked at Casey with complete confidence and sincerity. "Oh, Charlie comes right out and says he likes me," I said, causing both of them to laugh.

I was familiar with Charlie. We had a long friendship before it turned into more, and because of that, my mannerisms around him were completely comfortable. I sat next to him, and we smiled at each other before I leaned up and placed a quick kiss on his cheek.

"I'm telling AJ," Casey said, staring at us.

"Good, somebody needs to," Charlie returned, joking around.

"I will," I said with a shrug.

Charlie looked at me with a smile. His hand was on the key, and he went ahead and started the boat motor. I gave him another shrug, letting him know that I didn't care who knew about us, and he grinned at me as if he knew what I was saying. We didn't say anything else about it because Charlie turned the boat and headed onto the lake.

For the next couple of minutes, we didn't say anything at all. I sat next to him in the captain's seat, and we looked out at the water. He put his hand out once we were cruising, and I readily reached over for him. I leaned in to speak closer to his ear.

"I was sitting here thinking about your dad," I said.

"What about him?" Charlie asked.

Casey stared straight ahead from several feet in front of us, not paying attention or even hearing us.

"He came up to me in the house and said some really nice things just now. And, I don't know, he said that you liked me, and now I'm in a really good mood about it because it made me feel like he was okay with us seeing each other. It just feels good to know that he doesn't care if we date each other. You know, with the thing with my dad."

"I told you that was nothing to worry about," Charlie said.

"You did, but your dad was really nice about it just now, and it put me in a good mood. I feel like I want to climb Michael's Bluff about fifty times."

Charlie laughed and put his arm around me, rubbing my shoulder. I moved, leaning into him, getting comfortable.

We were still riding like that ten minutes later when we pulled around a bend and reached Michael's Bluff. I sat up and slipped out of Charlie's grasp once I knew we were in danger of being noticed. Charlie looked at me and smiled as he took my hand and placed it on his leg. He let go instantly so that he could tend to guiding the boat to a place near Max's bigger one. He wasn't holding onto me, and I could have easily withdrawn my hand, but I left it on his leg. I moved it slightly where it was in a little more discreet position, but I let my hand touch him as we pulled up next to his family.

AJ and Beau stood at the edge of the big boat looking down at us from their higher vantage point. Charlie knew how to maneuver on the water and the small boat approached the larger one gracefully in a side-by-side position. Casey stood up in preparation to act as a buffer for our boat.

Charlie moved to drop the anchor and AJ threw over a ladder. I knew we would climb up onto the larger boat with the others. Charlie and I broke contact in the process of pulling up but it was already too much for Casey.

"I know Hope was hanging out with you last year, AJ, but I think my brother is trying to score with her."

"Casey!" Charlie scolded his brother even though that was something we would all expect Casey to say.

"Yeah, you think so?" AJ said, sarcastically. We all glanced at him, and he gave us a sly grin and shrugged. "I figured it out the other day when I first got here, but then today she mentioned him about twenty times before he got here, and then he pulled up in the boat, and I watched her just jump off that cliff and float all the way over to him like she was full of helium." AJ motioned with his hand in the air as if I had jumped and floated in the air for a while before falling into the water, and everybody laughed, including me.

"I just jumped in the water—a regular jump," I defended, raising my hands and shaking my head.

"Yeah, but you jumped off of that cliff the second Charlie came around the corner, and then it took you about three seconds to swim over to him." He paused and made a dramatic face. "Then you guys took off together right after that. I think I did the math."

Chapter 20

Over two months later

I drove, and Landon rode in the front seat as we made our way to Stacy's restaurant. We weren't eating at The Black Skillet—we were only going there to pick up Stacy. We had plans to meet Charlie at the marina near the restaurant where we would get on his boat and travel over to the Morgan's house in Broken Arrow. Charlie was picking us up on the small boat since there were only three of us.

It was a going-away party of sorts. The three of us would be just about the only ones in attendance because most of the others in the Morgan family and all of the Camerons had already gone back to their respective cities weeks ago. Max, Charlie, and Caleb were the only ones still out at the property (not including my father, of course).

Max had stayed in Arkansas to see to his building project, and Charlie hung back with him. Caleb, Charlie's youngest brother, had come to Arkansas a week or so ago, and he arrived using a one-way plane ticket so that he could drive back to Florida with his dad and brother. They would be leaving to go back home to Miami tomorrow.

Charlie would go back to his normal life as a real estate developer in Miami. Only this time, he would have an extra companion. I would be leaving with them tomorrow, and I couldn't be more excited about it. Charlie and I had been spending all of our free time together, and we didn't have plans to stop. I was in love with him, and I felt empty when we weren't together. I had never been to Florida before, and I instantly agreed to move there with him when he asked me to. I had plans to live at Max's for now.

I grew up on the water obviously, so I was comfortable with that aspect of it, but palm trees and blue ocean water with salty sea air would be new to me. Charlie had shown me pictures and told me a lot of stories, so I knew what to expect somewhat, but I was still nervous and excited about going there with them. I couldn't wait to see it with my own two eyes. I had to put a significant amount of trust in Charlie to do this, though, which was why we had a certain wonderful, exciting conversation last night.

"We're getting married," I told Landon. "I'm going to marry him."

It was a huge piece of news in my life, and I delivered it nervously and quickly.

"I knew you would," Landon said, smiling and shaking his head at me. "I knew you were going to. Have you told your parents and brother?" he asked, looking at me from over the console.

"Just my mom, and that's because she came over today to help me pack. I haven't gone around calling anyone. It happened late last night, and I hardly believe it's real. It was just a conversation we had. I don't have a ring or anything. I'll tell my dad and Eric the first time I talk to them, I just had a lot going on today with packing and everything."

"What happened? How did it happen? How do you not have a ring? Did he forget it when he asked you?"

"No, he didn't forget, but it wasn't an official proposal in the way that you think of them on TV. We just got into a long conversation, and in it we decided to get married. It was just a conversation. Charlie wasn't prepared for it. Neither was I. He didn't have a ring. We just decided to get married."

"That sounds super romantic," Landon said. He was smiling and giving me a hard time, but he liked Charlie and he had been really nice about suddenly spending a lot less time with me.

"It was romantic, actually. I was glad he responded when I brought it up."

"You brought it up? You asked him? What did you say?"

"I said I didn't care about having a big proposal and we could and should just decide to get engaged. I want to marry him. I'm moving to a whole different state with him, so it feels right to get married."

I looked across the console at Landon. I was way more nervous about delivering the news of my engagement to my friends and family than I was about actually marrying Charlie, which was weird.

"Yeah," he said. "It might be a good idea to get engaged since you're moving and everything."

***

"Hope's getting married," Landon said ten minutes later when we walked into the bar at the restaurant and saw Stacy standing there.

She made a shocked face and gasped, hitting Landon on the shoulder as if he must be joking.

"I'm serious. She told me with her own mouth a few minutes ago, on the way over here. She said they decided to do it last night. Tell her, Hope."

"Well, I would have, but you already did," I said, looking at him with wide eyes like I was upset even though I really wasn't.

Stacy looked utterly shocked, staring at me.

"She said there's no ring or anything," Landon said. "It wasn't an official proposal."

"It was official," I said. "We said we decided to do it, and we talked about a date and everything."

"When? What date?" Stacy asked, still looking caught off guard.

"Christmas time. December. We'll do it here."

"This Christmas?" Stacy asked. "So, you know it? It's real? You're already engaged?"

"Yep. I know it. It's real. I'm engaged," I answered, smiling at her. I was confident about marrying Charlie, but I still couldn't shake the nerves associated with telling my friends. Stacy still looked shocked and dumbfounded, and Landon patted her on the shoulder and told her everything was going to be okay. She had taken the news fine when I told her I was moving to Miami, so I wasn't sure why this seemed like a bigger deal. Either way, I was completely comfortable with our decision to get married.

It was another ten minutes later when I got out of the car at the marina and figured out why Stacy was acting so funny. Charlie was at the marina in the big boat instead of the small one. There were ten or more people already on it. Caleb and Max were standing next to Charlie, they were the first ones I saw. My Brother, Eric, was there also, along with his girlfriend from Nashville. And that was when I started to know something was really going on. I started walking faster, going toward them while still scanning the crowd. My mom was there and so was my dad. I could see them all as we walked up, and my heart really started to pound. There were even a couple of my friends from work.

"My mother and father have not seen each other in years," I said to Landon and Stacy.

"I know. This is supposed to be a surprise," Stacy whispered stiffly as we walked up. "We didn't know about last night. We thought you were getting proposed to tonight."

"I think maybe I still am," I said, smiling at everyone on the boat.

I took a deep breath and turned to make eye contact with Charlie, who was looking back at me. I bit my lip and shook my head at him and he smiled.

I held my hands in the air as if to say *what's going on,* and he grinned even further and shrugged at me.

It only took a minute for us to reach the boat and begin to board it. I greeted my brother and talked about the amazing fact that he was finally back home. His girlfriend, Jillian, was with him, and I spoke with them briefly before looking around and greeting my mom and dad and the others.

"I know we all know why we're here," Charlie said at just the right time. He didn't raise his voice, but everyone knew he was trying to get our attention, and we went silent and looked at him, waiting to hear what he would say next.

He moved to stand closer to me and we converged and got settled near the edge of the boat. "I did not come to Arkansas to fall in love," he said. "I came here to run from it—to heal from it. I certainly wasn't looking for it." He looked at me. "Hope wasn't either. When we first started spending time together, we were friends with neither of us wanting anything else. I was the one who fell first. I had to talk her into this."

Everyone laughed when he said that and I defended him. "Aw, you didn't have to try too hard."

They all reacted. They made various noises like they thought we were sweet. Charlie took me into his arms and then continued speaking.

"As you all know, I planned this last week, but then Hope and I decided to get married last night, so technically, I've already asked her. We love each other very much and we know this is the right thing to do. In our conversation last night, she specifically told me that she didn't care about a traditional engagement. She said she would not know what to do if I got on my knees and held up a ring box. She actually used the word mortified in that conversation, so I'm not going to kneel... but..." Charlie took a box out of his pocket and held the closed box comfortably in front of us like he wasn't in a rush for me to take it from him. "I'm going to make this quick okay, my love? I love you. I love your memory, and your empathy, and your way with kids. My heart is more full of love today than it has ever been in my life. I know we already decided that we were getting married and you didn't expect any of this, but I already had it planned, and I wanted to have everyone here when I gave you this. So, here. And since you've already said *yes*, you can just smile and kiss me now."

Epilogue

The following December

I was standing in my gazebo.

It was everyone's gazebo, but Max referred to it as mine because it was built as a surprise to me for our wedding which was a week ago. It was an exact replica of the one that had been at my apartment complex, only better. It was beautifully built, and they positioned it on the perfect piece of land where you could see the house and the dock, but you were also shrouded by some woods. They had nestled it in the midst of some of my favorite trees. I had been standing in it for ten or fifteen minutes, having memories about our wedding and about our first kiss in the other, very similar gazebo. It was cool out, and I was all alone, looking out at the quiet lake and having a quiet moment.

My dad had helped build it.

He had bragged to me about it.

Charlie hired an expert carpenter. The man worked with an assistant, but my dad volunteered to help them, carrying and stacking wood and doing other odd jobs for the two of them. We were away in Miami when it was being built, and my father came to me and told me all about it when we got here and Charlie surprised me with it.

My father had carried wood.

He had lugged wood from one place to another, and he was feeling overjoyed to tell me this information. He was proud to tell me he carried the wood that made this, and I felt tears come to my eyes as I looked at it and imagined him laboring. My dad was honored to carry the wood that built this beautiful structure. He had chosen to work hard for a cause he believed in, and he was proud of the results. He had been willing to serve in whatever capacity he was needed, and it was important to him that I knew he had been a part of it.

In that moment, I understood the concept Ms. Bridgette was trying to get across to me that day. I appreciated the whole thing on a spiritual level, and it caused hot tears to continue gathering in my eyes. I stood back, stepping into the middle of the structure and looking upward to stop tears from falling. It was a well-built gazebo that put the one at my old apartment complex to shame. Charlie had hired a gardener to transplant flowers and vines, and it looked like it had been here for years. I stood there feeling thankful.

Tears were still gathered in my eyes when I heard Charlie whistle. I blinked and peered into the yard. He was standing near the house, and he waved at me.

I gestured at him to come over, and he smiled and began to jog my way. A smile covered my face at the sight of my husband. There was a wide-open space of yard between us, and I stood there in the shade and watched him jog toward me. He had a long, athletic stride, and he easily ran over to me, smiling. He was wearing jeans and a hoodie with tennis shoes and he ran up to me easily.

I moved to the edge of the doorway and waited there for him. Charlie did not stop or even slow down until he reached me. He ran right up to me, touching and kissing me the instant we were close enough. His hands reached out for mine and we were all of a sudden mouth to mouth.

"Mmm, hello," I said.

"Hello."

"Your brother is going to the hospital," he said casually.

"What? Are you serious? He woke up? What'd he say? It still hurts?"

My brother and Jillian had come to Arkansas for the wedding, and they would be here until after Christmas. My brother got along really well with the Morgans, and he and Jillian spent about half of their time (including some nights) out here at the big house with us.

My brother was a decent skateboarder, and he loved the Morgan's house for skating. They had a long, smooth driveway at the front entrance, with some stairs and paths with inclines that were perfect for skating. That was exactly how he had hurt his shoulder. Last I heard, he took some ibuprofen and he and Julian were going to take a nap to see if he could sleep it off.

"He's just going to have it x-rayed," Charlie said. He pulled me further into the gazebo.

"Where are we going?" I asked.

"Back here. You're the one who called me over here."

"Does Eric need me?" I asked.

He shook his head as he sat down and pulled me onto his lap. "He's fine. He's just going to have an x-ray, just in case. Beau had a similar injury from Lacrosse. They were talking about it. He said Eric probably just needs physical therapy. Eric is just going to check it out. Jillian's driving him. They're going down to Little Rock. They probably already left. He told me to tell you. I knew I'd find you out here."

"I didn't think I had been out here that long. I didn't know Eric was awake or that you were finished with your phone calls."

Charlie pulled me in and got me settled on his lap with my legs over his on the bench seat of the gazebo. I wasn't comfortable resting my weight on my own shins, so I sat back, sitting directly on his lap. My body responded to him and I kissed him, shifting my weight to get closer and hold onto him.

Charlie let out a small groan. "If there weren't ten other people at this house, Hope..." Charlie didn't finish his sentence because both of us knew exactly what he was going to say. I leaned down and kissed him again, moving slowly. I touched him carefully. I reached out and put my hands on his face.

"Your eyes are watering," he said, staring at me. "Are you okay?"

I nodded. "I'm amazing. It was happiness. I was thinking about this gazebo."

"I get lucky in gazebos," Charlie said, using my shirt to pull me into another kiss.

His kiss was so scorching hot that I broke away from him saying, "Charlieeee."

He grinned and then made a regretful face. "Uhh, I'm really tired suddenly. All those emails and phone calls… It's nice out here, but I'm going inside, into the privacy of the guesthouse, to take a nap."

"Yeah, I'm actually really tired, too," I said. "I think I'm going to take a nap as well. That sounds like a great idea."

Charlie grinned and moved to stand up and I smiled back as I followed his lead. Both of us began walking toward the house, and neither of us bothered to clarify that we were just joking about the nap.

The End
(till book 2)

Thanks to my team ~ Chris, Coda, Jan, Glenda, and Yvette